CW01498222

Hunter

I have a secret. One that will change everything. I made a deal, one I wont back out of. Only time has run out, and they will all know soon enough.

Jace

She forgave me…but it's not a simple as "I'm sorry." I'm used to saying those words and all is forgiven. But this is Mila Hart… nothing's ever gonna be easy with her. And I wouldn't have it any other way.

Roman

I made a mess of my life before she came back, and it follows me still. Only now. I'm not alone fighting my demons and I have something worth fighting for.

Mila

Freaking butterflies…

THE GAME

REBELS OF RIDGECREST HIGH #3

BELLE HARPER

ONE
ASHER

uck!

Everything's fucked.

That first day I met Mila Hart, I knew she was going to be a problem. Hell, she wasn't what I had been expecting at all. I knew then I was in trouble.

She's gorgeous, and she doesn't even have to try. It's just who she is. She could be wearing that tiny little bikini in my hot tub or an oversized hoodie while stuffing her face with popcorn on the sofa. Either way, she's beautiful. Mila has that girl-next-door vibe; she makes sweet and charming seem effortless.

But her no shits given, smart mouth, princess attitude, that's what sealed the deal. I love it, even though I shouldn't. I never wanted to feel this way about anyone. Didn't want what my parents had. Their marriage and divorce swore me off relationships. I keep my heart locked tight. But a little blonde firecracker—who cockblocked me within an hour of our meeting—has wormed her way in, and I want to keep her.

I do, and that's the dilemma.

I wish she was a bitch from New York. I wish she wasn't the daughter of James...the only reason I even know her is because her dad is dating Mom. I wouldn't have met her otherwise. Okay, I might have seen her at a Rebels game or a party. I never would have gotten to know her. We might have hooked up for a night, and that would be the end of it. I wouldn't feel like this about her because I wouldn't have *known* the real her.

I'd been straight-up honest with Mila when I said I didn't have sisterly thoughts of her that first day. She cockblocked me. I agreed to it, thinking this was just some physical attraction and that it meant nothing. Well, I was wrong.

The no fucking each other rule...what dumbass agreed to that?

Yeah, that rule made sense, for all of a week, maybe. That's how long it took me to realize it's not only physical, but this girl has also gotten under my skin. Everything she does, every time I see or think of her, makes my heartbeat that little bit faster. I love the way she pushes my buttons, constantly messing around and testing my limits. She's always herself. She never pretends to be something different.

Mila teases and flirts, but it's always with the understanding that nothing's going to happen. I tease and flirt with her just as much as she does me, but there's a safety barrier between us. We already have the rule in place, which makes it easier to be myself and drop my guard, since I don't have to impress her. We know it's just a game. At least it was at the start.

She's forbidden and off-limits. Same for me where she's concerned. Only, we made the rules to this game, so we can break them.

It's all fun and games until one of us catches feelings, and I didn't expect it to be me. She has a boyfriend…hell, she has two, and I don't even get how that works, but I'm a jealous mess. I like Hunter—he's fun and a good guy. But now, every time I see him with Mila, I want to punch his smug smile right off his face. Fucker got the girl. *My girl.*

He knows I have a thing for Mila. Hell, he probably figured it out before I did. He hasn't said anything to me since I walked in on them that morning, and I acted like a complete asshole. I guess he feels safe since she's always loved him; I can't compete with him. He doesn't view me as a threat.

Not like Roman. He sees me as someone who will take her away. I don't know him well, but I can tell he would fight to the death before losing Mila. She would do the same for him. Hell, she went to save Roman from his abusive dad and ended up killing the man in self-defense.

I'd like to think I can handle myself in a fight. I work out and keep fit for football. But Roman is bigger, quicker, and stronger than me. I wouldn't stand a chance if he saw me as a threat and wanted to eliminate me.

"Asher, what's wrong?" Mom asks.

I look up from my now-cold meal. Everyone at the dinner table is watching me…well, almost everyone. Mila's beside me and looking anywhere but at me.

Fuck, I can't even get through a meal without obsessing over her.

She smells like roses today, a new perfume. I haven't smelled that one on her before. *Fuck*, what's wrong with me? I need to get over her. Over whatever this is between us…well, what I feel.

I let out a deep breath and shrug, "nothing." A cryptic answer.

Something mom isn't used to from me. As she tilts her head and questions me with her eyes, I look away, unable to lie to her. She can see right through me, and I hope she drops this. But I have a feeling that, when we're alone, she'll ask me again, and I don't want to tell her what's really wrong. She will have to deal with "nothing" as an answer for a long time.

"I just want to ask," James starts, and I look over at him. His eyes met mine then dart to Mila. *Fuck*. Does he know? Can he see right through me. "Did you have a fight? Is there something upsetting you both? You haven't been yourselves in weeks."

How do I answer that? *Yeah, well, weeks ago, I did something dumb by telling your daughter I want her and messed up what we had, and I don't know if I can fix it or if I even want it to go back to the way it was before.*

I don't think I can answer. I fucked up everything by admitting my feeling, something I've never done before, and I did it in the worst way possible. I'm angry and irritated at myself for being such an asshole about it. That's not what I wanted. I wanted to tell her I like her and ask her out on a date. But I was too late to tell her. She has Hunter now.

I was angry at Hunter for beating me to it and myself for waiting so long to tell her. Then angry at myself for thinking I even stood a chance against him and their history.

I never did.

I never will.

So instead, I try and push down these feelings, but they continue to simmer just below the surface. But it's clear, I'm not being careful enough. James and Mom are seeing right through my fake smiles and quiet head nods.

"No, Dad," Mila answers. "We didn't have a fight. I've just had a lot on my mind with everything, and it's exhausting trying to catch up on all of my work."

James nods slightly. "Maybe you shouldn't see Hunter and Roman as much. Then, you will have a chance to catch up. I will call the school and explain why you need more time.

"You can take all the time you need, sweetheart. They need understand that you will be behind after what happened."

I perk up—that's a great idea. If she sees Hunter and Roman less, I could help her with her homework and maybe fix what's broken between us.

When Mila shifts slightly, her arm brushes mine. My breath hitches slightly, and she pulls it back just as fast. My chest grows heavy. I did this. I messed up everything.

What we had before was amazing, and I miss it that now I don't have it. I would rather be heartbroken and still have the flirty, fun Mila than what I have now. I miss the way she would always come find me first when she came over to the house. The way she would flop onto my bed and poke my ribs and tell me silly jokes. The way she laughed at my dumb jokes and bad flirting.

"I can help with your work. I'm a great tutor," I blurt out.

Mom's brows raise, as if she has just caught me in a lie, but then I see her smile and nod.

"No," Mila whips out quickly, then straightens up beside me. "I mean, no thank you, I'm fine. Hunter has been helping me. He knows the work already, since we go to the same school and have the same classes."

Well, I read that loud and clear. Just like a stab to the heart.

"What do you mean you're going to crash a Rebels Halloween party?" Walker yells as he turns to me from the passenger seat of my car. He flicks his eye patch up to glare at me better, and I roll my eyes.

"I'm not crashing… I just wasn't officially invited." I whisper the last part under my breath.

So what if I wasn't invited? I know Emerson Henty is throwing it and that Mila will be there. I saw what she was wearing earlier, and I just… I need to see her. I need to apologize to her. To Hunter and Roman. Fuck, I have no plans going into this. All I know is that I have to see her and make this right.

"I thought we were going to Melissa's. I had that hot dancer from Royale Academy all lined up for tonight." He huffs.

Crossing his arms against his chest, he sags into the leather seat. I don't say anything; I just continue with my stupid plan.

He sits up, running his hand over his face and shakes his head. "I love you, man, you know that, but fuck. You need to give her up. You told her how you feel, and you fucked that up by spending the entire night drowning yourself in any alcohol you could get your hands on. Then you passed out on the recliner downstairs.

"I'm sure Tanner loved that, though. He took the room I gave you and hooked up with Trisha. Lucky son of a bitch." Walker shakes his head and whistles lowly.

I don't want to hear what he's got to say next because I know what happened. *I was there.*

"You were still drunk when you went charging in there. Trying to be what? A knight who smelled like sweat and booze and rescue her from her boyfriend—who I happen to like, and I thought you did too. Hunter's a good guy, and as much as I want to be your friend and say positive things, I can't, man. You don't stand a chance against him. Mila and him, their history. They're the type of couple you see in movies. Endgame shit. White picket fence and kids, man."

"I want that," I mutter. I do. With Mila.

"Look, think about it this way. She cockblocked you, she is probably gonna be your stepsister, and I still think you want her because she is the one girl who won't fall at your feet. You used to be a player at parties, but when was the last time you got laid?"

"Fuck you." I grip the steering wheel a little tighter.

"Exactly. Fuck… some chick. Preferably tonight, so you can stop this shit. She's there with them, you know. This isn't the fairy tale. She isn't gonna run at you with her arms wide and declare she loves you. She's gonna be all loved up with Hunter and Roman. Her boyfriend's. So, let's turn around and go to Melissa's."

I roll my head from side to side; my neck is tight, and I'm anxious. I'd hoped to have Walker on my side. Hunter's a good guy—I'm not denying it—but I need to do this. I have to fix this now before I go home, even if I have to lie to make this weirdness stop. Looking out to the road in front of me, I let out a deep breath and shake my head.

"I know, but I just… you don't get it, okay? I need to fix this. I need to tell her that I take it all back. She doesn't feel the same way, and I want us to be like we were." I miss that. Being so honest and telling her all my secrets. I loved having someone to confide in.

He doesn't speak again; he just sits there, tapping away at his phone, as I head toward the party we weren't invited to. When Mila sees me there… I don't know what I'll say first or how I'm going to say it. Will she realize I'm there for her, that I want to fix whatever this is between us?

I'll have to pretend that I'm not falling in love with her. That I want to be friends and spend time with her like we used to. Even if I have to watch her all coupled up with Hunter and Roman. Hell, I want to ask her what that's about and how it works. Maybe there's room for me? But how? I can't without sounding like a jealous asshole, and I don't want to be that.

"I gave Hunter a heads-up, but you need to stop this after tonight. Find another girl, and fuck Mila out of your system. There are plenty of girls waiting for us at Melissa's, so go, say you're sorry, then let's go get some pussy. Hell, I'll even let you have the hot dancer."

My fingers tighten around the steering wheel. I don't want some hot dancer. Walker doesn't get it, but I can't blame him. I'd be acting the same way in his shoes. I didn't know that you could feel this way about someone. He doesn't get that I just can't fuck Mila out of my system. That's not how this works. At least, it's not going to work for me.

Until I get over this, I will continue torturing myself around her. I keep telling myself she won't meet my eyes because she feels something too, and the moment she does, she'll give in and kiss me.

What the fuck is wrong with me? I'm acting like a character in one of Mom's sappy Christmas romances that she watches year-round with Madison. I might have accidentally sat down and watched a few of them too. But it's not that simple. That shit isn't real. She isn't a city girl from New York while I'm some small-town country boy that she doesn't even know she needed in her life. She was here before... she has an entire past that will give her the happily ever after. And I'm going to be the side character, time and time again.

I pull up on Emerson's street. It's packed with cars, but I find us a spot and quickly park. This party has been going for hours already, and a lot of partygoers are out on the street.

It's a different type of neighborhood than I'm used to visiting. Though it's similar to James and Mila's street, the lawns aren't mowed, and the houses are lacking basic care. It's amazing how the scenery changes in just a few blocks. But people have lives here. No need to be an asshole about their houses.

I'm dressed in a skeleton outfit. Madison did an amazing job painting my face. I don't look like me; I could be anyone. Well, at least, I feel like I won't be recognized at this party. I'll blend in. That's what I love about Halloween.

Grabbing my black baseball cap, I push it down over my hair. Walker just stares at me and rolls his eyes. I shove his shoulder, then I get out and close my door before stretching and looking around. Yeah, this might not be the best area to park my BMW. Not judging… okay, I'm being an asshole.

"They'll know it's you as soon as we go in. You're here with me." Walker points to himself.

He's right. They will know if I go with him. Walker isn't one to blend with the crowd. He was born to stand out. "Go in without me. I want to be invisible."

Walker gives me a pitying look, then flicks his eyepatch back over his right eye and raises his plastic sword in the air with a stupid grin and fake pirate voice. "Argh, my boney friend. I shall take all the sexy wenches for my own while you pine over one."

I can't help but smile. Walker's always good at lightening up the mood. He knows I hate when he flirts nonstop with Mila, but he's a good friend most the time.

"I only need one, pirate. Have fun, and don't get scurvy or any other diseases."

Walker shuffles his feet backward and spins, then does some fancy footwork and stabs me in the stomach with his stupid sword. He chuckles then runs off to the house, stabbing everyone he passes. They know who he is as soon as they see him. He loves all the attention, good and bad.

I slink around the side of the house, avoiding as many people as I can, which is easy. They're drunk or making out back here. I make my way into the backyard and look for her… and she isn't hard to find.

TWO
MILA

To say I'm not nervous would be a lie.

We came to Emerson's Halloween party tonight in the hopes we could be normal. Normal teens going to a costume party with friends. But no one, apart from the three of us, knows the truth. Roman is fighting for the Amato family. Hunter goes to all his fights to help keep him safe, and I hide at Kate's place while they're both gone so they don't have to worry about me. Jace has no idea that's why Roman's still fighting.

Jace has no idea what's really happening.

He doesn't know what happened with my "accident," and he doesn't know who really killed Damon. He doesn't know we're keeping this colossal lie that has the three of us all twisted up inside and always looking over our shoulders. We have to tell him. He needs to know, in case he gets caught up in all of it. Our web of lies grows and only puts others in danger.

But how? How do you tell someone that your

slowly trusting again, that you didn't kill someone? That you took the fall to keep your best friend safe? How can you trust he won't use that against you or tell the wrong person when he's angry and mad? Jace is a wild card right now and one I won't show my entire hand to. *Not yet.*

If Roman doesn't fight and lose or win for the Amato family, they will come for me. Hurt me again. Hunter's so involved now, he fumbled the ball in last night's game, causing the Rebels to lose so Coach won't pull Roman from first string.

I tug the hem of my red dress again, and Roman grabs my wrist to stop me. I know what he's thinking. The old me wouldn't be fidgeting and looking over my shoulder every few minutes. Always watching my surroundings and what's lurking in the dark. But I keep on doing just that. Without realizing it, I'm giving away little tells that something isn't right, and Roman picks up on them. Hell, even Jace mentioned that I've changed. I'm different.

We've all changed. He thinks it's because of what happened in the trailer, with Damon's death. We don't correct him. I have changed, but it's not because of that or what he thinks I did.

I lace my fingers into Roman's hand, and I can feel all eyes on me. They watch and wait. So many people from school want to know what's happening between the three of us. I love to watch their faces light up with excitement and then fall in disappointment when all we do is hold hands. It's a fun little game for me, and right now, I could use all the fun I can get.

I'm saving my kisses for Roman until we're behind closed doors. Not that I'm hiding him like he's a secret, but he doesn't like to let his guard down. Kissing me out here in public would mean he's not watching for danger. Hunter would have to take over in that department, and well, Hunter gets distracted easily… and drunk like he is now. But he needed a night off. Roman does too, but he won't, even for a night, and I hate that. You would think that, after the death of his father, things would have improved, but they have only gotten more complicated.

"Devil girl, light a fire in my pants and spank me." I hear a deep chuckle and turn to the voice I know so very well.

Walker Murphy is standing there with a cocky grin on his face and dressed as a pirate. He waves his plastic sword in the air, and I try to hide the smile forming on my face. He looks good. And he knows it.

"That's a big sword, Walker. Trying to compensate for something?" I tease and cock my hip. He just winks and grabs his crotch.

"Two swords are better than one. You, of all people, should know that." He winks then points his plastic sword to Hunter, who's playing beer pong with Jace and Emerson, then points it to where I'm holding Roman's hand. He looks at me and winks again before chuckling.

I tilt my head and raise my eyebrows, challenging him to say something. I'm not giving Walker anything. He's asked a few times what's between the three of us, but I won't give him a straight answer and it's driving him crazy. He knows, but he wants me to say it. We stare at each other, neither of us backing down.

Roman's hold on my hand tightens. He doesn't like Walker much or Asher. *Asher*. I break my gaze from Walker and look around, but I don't see Asher. Weren't they supposed to be going to some Lakeview party? Some girl's house? Not that I was listening earlier or even cared where he went at all. He can go to Melissa's party if he wants to.

"I guess since you won't tell me what the deal is with you three, I won't tell you if *he* is or isn't here." Walker smirks.

Fuck. Am I that obvious?

I take a step into Roman. He stiffens a little, but I don't know if it's from me touching him or what Walker just said.

"I wasn't looking for him," I say too late, and Walker just shakes his head and sighs.

"If you say so, Miss Mila. I'm gonna get some beer. You want anything?" Walker offers. He's trying to be friendly with Roman, but when Roman doesn't reply, I shake my head.

With a nod, he turns around and puts on that Walker charm thick. "Hey, ladies, who wants to do shots and play with my sword?"

A few girls bat their eyes at him and giggle. I let out a little snort when one wraps her arm around his waist. He glances back and winks at me. Then his eyes dart to something to the side of the house, and he lifts his chin in a nod.

I follow his gaze to a skeleton standing there in the

dark. The light from the back porch shines just enough for me to know it's Asher. Why's he standing over there all alone? He gestures for me to come over to him. Is he serious?

"What does he want?" Roman growls low in my ear.

I shake my head and turn to look up at Roman, placing my hand very gently on his cheek. His eyes soften, and I know he's only worked up because he cares about me.

But he doesn't know what Asher said to me. I haven't found the time to tell him and Hunter. Okay, that's a lie. But how do you tell the two guys you love, that share you because you can't choose between them, that your kind-of stepbrother admitted he has feelings, and you've worked out that you also have feelings for him, and it freaks you out? *A lot.*

"I don't know or care what he wants."

Roman grunts, and I know he can read right through that lie. I'm trying to tell myself that I don't care, so I won't think about Asher. It's not working. I shake my head, and Roman's lip tilts a little at the corner as he looks over my head toward Asher.

"Go see what he wants." He lets go of my hand, and I turn, letting out a deep breath as I pull on the hem of my dress again. I hear the deep rumble from Roman and let go of the hem once more.

My fingers clenching into fists as I walk over to Asher on what feels like unsteady feet. It's dark where he waits, not many people nearby, but Roman's watching me. There's no way he would have let me go here alone if he couldn't see me.

"What are you doing here?" I left my phone in Hunter's car. I just wanted to switch off for a while, but now I'm worried something happened and that's why he's here.

Asher's eyes land on mine, and my heart races as butterflies dance in my belly. I haven't looked at him in weeks. Okay, another lie. Might as well keep going. I have so many now, I'm starting to confuse what's truth from fiction.

I've looked at him, trying to work out if the butterflies are real. I've only had butterflies for three people in my life... well, four. *Grady*. I experienced one little butterfly for him once, but that's nothing compared to the ones I have for Asher. With Hunter and Roman, it's very clear what I truly feel for them. Jace... his butterflies are still there, but there are less of them now. Hiding from the hurt.

Asher's face is painted in shades of black, white, and gray. It looks unreal. His big, dark eyes move behind me, and he shifts his weight on his feet. It's been a month since he told me he has feelings for me. Exactly to the day. He hasn't been the same since. Hell, neither have I, but to be honest, I miss the old, flirty Asher. He was funny and confident and now he's... well, this. Avoiding me and barely speaking a word to me. And I've been acting the same way.

"Asher? Are you okay?" I ask when he doesn't answer me.

"No. Yes. Depends." He looks at me, and I raise my eyebrows.

I'm not ready for him to tell me he has feelings for

me again, so I hope that isn't what this is about. I shake my hands out. *Not now.* There's too much going on, and this is a huge complication. He can't tell Hunter and Roman what he told me. I need to tell them both myself, and soon, because this secret is growing each day, and it's going to mess up everything I've built with them.

"Asher?" I prod. Roman will only wait so long before he comes over here.

"Punishment."

Fuck. I stand taller and look him right in the eye.

"Why do you need to punish yourself?" I feel like I'm torturing him every time I'm around, because that's how it feels when he's around me.

"Because I fucked up the one good thing I had, and I don't know how to fix it. How to get back to what we had before. I want to take back what I said. I fucked up, and hurt you in the process. I miss you. What we had… I miss that. The laughter, the jokes. I didn't realize how much I need you in my life until now. I'm sorry, Mila."

My heart races. He's sorry. He wants to take it back. This is a good thing. But how can we go back to the way we were? We can't just switch this off. It happened *because of* what we had before. If we go back to that, it's only going to grow and grow. Do I want that? No? Yes? Maybe? *I don't know.*

"You don't have feelings for me anymore?" I'm confused more than ever now.

He doesn't say anything. Instead, he shuffles a little and peers over my shoulder to Roman. I turn and see

Roman watching us. He nods slightly, and I look back to Asher. His hands are in his pockets now and he looks smaller, defeated. I hate that I'm causing him this pain.

"No." He looks away as he says it. When I don't respond, he shake his head. "Look, I get it. I don't have a chance with you. I will get over my feelings. But can we go back to being friends? Please."

That should make me happy, it's one last thing I need to worry about. But why does it feel like someone's twisting a knife in my chest? And why do I feel like bursting into tears? PMS. Blame it on good old PMS. Except, I'm not due for my period anytime soon. *Ugh...* why is this so hard. Why does my heart beat for more than one? I have a very greedy heart, that's for sure.

But Asher's giving me an out, and I have to take it. I know I should just tell him that he isn't alone in his feelings. But what does he want me to do about them? I have two amazing boyfriends, already. Where would Asher fit into the equation if I did act on my feelings? Is it only because we have gotten so close? Would they go away over time? I don't know the answers to these questions.

Roman wraps his arm around my waist and I startle a little. I can't overthink this anymore. If being friends is what Asher wants, it's what I can give him.

"Friends." I put my hand out for him to shake, and he takes it in his warm one. I feel it throughout my whole body. *Butterflies.*

There's a pause where our shake goes on longer

than it should, and Roman makes a sound in the back of his throat.

"Friends," Asher repeats.

"Perfect." I nod. "Friends," I repeat again, as if I need to hear that word one more time. Just to make sure it sinks in… *friends.* Such a simple word.

But when it comes to Asher, it's never going to be simple.

THREE
JACE

Another day of school and things are weird.

I knew they would be, after everything that happened between us all. Mila forgiving me was a huge step forward, especially after I verbally attacked her over killing Roman's dad. That wasn't fair of me. But she forgave me, and I'm so grateful. But things are weird, now that they're all together and dating and I'm left on the sidelines watching. I don't know how to get past that. We used to do everything together, but now I feel like the fourth wheel, and I hate it.

I don't want to watch without being able to join in. I want to be with Mila. But I don't know how I would even fit in, if she let me. She said we all give her butterflies, and she won't choose. Hunter agreed to that, and so did Roman. I don't completely understand their relationship. In public, Mila and Hunter are all over each other… it's disgusting sometimes. But with Roman, it's different. Mila only holds hands with him. But everyone's watching and waiting. I know better. I have seen them together, and I don't like the jealously that rises inside me, wishing it was me.

I guess this is what I've always feared. Being left out. The pact was meant to stop this from happening to two of us, but because I'm a prick who went into a jealous rage, there's now only one left out. *Me*. The one who set the stupid childhood pact into motion and reminded them all the day she got back, and now I'm paying for it. For being greedy.

Hunter already had a conversation with me before I apologized to Mila. He told me how he and Roman are both with her. That, if I have an issue, to go and fuck myself. So I'm keeping my jealously to myself and going with whatever they throw at me, because what else can I do? I don't want to be left out anymore.

I'm envious. It seems so natural for them. They aren't jealous of each other, and they don't seem to fight over her attention. I don't know how they do it. I would be a mess if I was Hunter or Roman. I've always dreamed that she would be mine and mine alone. I know that can't happen now, and I've accepted that.

This is the way it is, and to be honest, it's the only way it would have ever worked. No one is left out… well, when she finally lets me in, that is.

But I keep how much I want to be with her to myself. My big mouth and my actions got me here on the sidelines. This is my punishment for being an asshole, and the only way I can get back what we once had is to show her I've changed.

I thought it would be like old times with the three of

them. Just hanging out and having fun. But that's not the case, at all.

Watching Hunter kiss Mila, wishing those were my lips on hers. Yeah, I can deal with that. I fucked up. But then, watching Roman devour her, and when her eyes meet mine, it makes me wish I were next. That she would come to me and kiss me. But she doesn't, and I know she's punishing me for what I did with Britney. It was a low blow and one I wish I could take back.

The fact that they're together, I can deal with that. It's the whispering to each other when I'm around and always feeling left out I can't deal with.

They have secrets, and they don't want to share them with me. They whisper, and if I get too close, they stop or, a few times, I picked up the name Amato. I don't like the way my friends don't trust me enough to talk to me about it.

let out a deep breath as I round the corner to the school office. My nose scrunches at the sight of Britney Montlake staring at me from where she stands. Her hip rests against the desk, and she's wearing dark jeans and a red top that makes her red, pouty lips bigger than they are. And not in a good way.

"I know you're ignoring me, but soon you won't be. The truth will come out, and your friends will all be in prison, and I'm all you will have left."

The fuck? I've been called to the principal's office and wasn't sure why, but seeing her here is bad news.

Then I see him—my dad. He's here too. He's talking to the office assistant, and when he catches my eyes, I freeze. What's this about?

I glare at Britney and grit my teeth. "What. Did. You. Do?" I ground out, and she just smiles and winks.

None of this makes sense. Is this about Grady? With my dad involved, it has to be. But Grady isn't here. And why would my friends be going to prison? Britney should be the one doing time for what she did to Grady. I was the shitty boyfriend; I was the one who treated her badly, and my brother's the one who paid for it.

"Fuck you, bitch," I growl lowly enough for just her to hear me, but her expression doesn't change. She merely tilts her head as if she hasn't heard me.

The door to the principal's office opens, but it's not Mrs. Hadley. It's a cop with a big belly, almost popping buttons off his uniform. I have a perfect donut joke for him, but I don't know what this is about, so I keep my mouth shut.

"Jace Montero?" he asks, and I nod as I look around, trying to figure out what this is about. "Come inside."

My feet feel glued to the floor. I don't want to go in there. I don't know what he has to say, but I've heard enough. My dad comes up behind me, and his hand on my back has me moving forward. He shakes the officer's hand as I stand there confused.

"And I'm Daniel Montero, Jace's father."

The cop nods and ushers us into the office. I turn to see Britney with a huge grin on her face just as another officer closes the door. He's a big man, and I recognize that face. It's Britney's dad. *Fuck sake.*

"Take a seat, please. It's nice to see you again, Daniel. It's been a while." He shakes my father's hand. They know each other because of my former relationship with Britney. "We have some questions we would like to ask you, Jace."

I keep standing and cross my arms. Fuck this shit. I did nothing wrong, and if Britney put them up to this, I'm gonna kill her.

I look at Dad, but he just shakes his head and gestures for me to sit.

"Jace, we would like to talk to you about Mila Hart, Roman Valentine, and Hunter West." *What?* I look at the big-bellied cop and back to my dad.

"Take a seat, boy." Officer Montlake's voice grows louder. He isn't asking.

Dad's eyes meet mine, and they plead for me to sit. Not to cause a scene. My arms drop to my sides and my hands fist. I don't like the way this cop is asking about my friends.

The cops bringing me in here can't be good for Mila and the guys. My heart races, and a wave of cold rushes through me as my stomach drops.

It's got to be about Mila killing Roman's dad. It has to be. What did Britney say to her dad to get them here, questioning me at school?

I know Mila's been making Britney's life a living hell after what she did to Grady. But Britney's a bitch and has been calling her names like "killer."

"As you know, there was an incident involving the three of them recently. And I have it on good authority that you were friends with them up until a few weeks before this happened. Is that correct?" the other cop asks.

I look back to the closed door, as though I can see Britney standing there with that grin on her face. It was an accident. It was self-defense. I never asked Mila directly, but I know she wouldn't have killed Roman's dad if she had any other choice. For me to be here, questioned by the cops…

What did I say when I was angry and venting my shit out loud with Britney around? She's angry and just trying to get back at me. That's all this is. Just a fallen queen trying to regain her crown.

I sit up straighter. "Why do you have me here?"

"We are looking into an ongoing investigation. One that involves your three friends. And we have questions for you," Officer Montlake explains. And he would know… he knew me growing up. He knew us all.

"We've had a witness come forward with some information, and we need you to tell us what you know about the incident that resulted in the death of Mr. Damon Valentine."

I shake my head. "I don't know anything about it. I wasn't there."

"Well, I don't know. You have always been thick as thieves, you four. I would find it highly unlikely you don't know *anything*."

I don't answer; I just sit there silently. I don't know anything, and I'm not about to talk. I'm not stupid.

The other cop starts speaking, and I try to ignore him until he asks a question that I've been asking myself. "What's their association with the Amato Family?"

When my eyes find the officer, he tilts his head and smiles. I curse myself. *Fuck.*

Amato. I've heard the three of them use that name a few times while whispering. I googled it and it came up with the Amato crime family and I knew that had to be wrong, but for him to ask this. It can't be wrong. And I just said without words, that they have a connection to this family. *Fuck.* I don't say anything, and he stares me down.

"Tell us about their relationship," Officer Montlake says. "There's some talk about the three of them being all involved with each other… sexually. But Jace, you're not involved with them sexually?"

My eyes meet his, and I narrow them. This fucker has gone too far. I edge forward, and I can see the smile forming on his face. He knows I'm left out. He would have gotten that much from Britney and is trying to play it, so I will rise and talk. I tend to get angry and run my mouth. Not anymore.

"I wasn't aware this was what you were going to be asking when you called us down here," Dad tells them both. "You haven't even read my son his rights. If you want to ask any more questions, you can ask through our lawyer." He stands and I do too. Officer Montlake watches me as I leave the office.

"You will hear from our lawyer," Dad says as he closes the door on them and takes my arm, leading me away from the room.

We walk away until we're out of earshot, and Dad

turns to me. "Never talk to them without a lawyer. I don't know what they're after. That thing with Mila, it was self-defense, so I don't understand what's happening right now, but don't speak to them. They can twist words. Go home, and I'll meet you there. First, I'm going to call James and let him know the police are questioning you."

Dad leaves, and I stand there, trying to wrap my head around what just happened. I didn't even know we had a lawyer. But I'm smart enough to know that I need to keep my mouth shut and not speak to the police again without one. I could say one thing, and they will twist it to make it fit whatever agenda they have.

"So, do you trust your so-called friends? Have they told you the truth of what *really* happened?"

I spin to face Britney. She just won't give up. Or give me up as she traces a finger up my arm, and I bat her arm away. She pouts her red lips. Ugh, why did I ever fuck her in the first place? I never should have gone out with her; she just won't leave me alone.

"What do you know that you're not telling me?" If she'd overheard her father, I want to know, and maybe she will tell me. Like why they're still investigating this. This is bullshit. Self-defense, they said it was. So, what's got them asking questions now?

"Not what I heard… what I *saw*." She smirks and turns on her heel and walks away, swinging her hips as she leaves.

I stand there, rolling her words around in my head. Not what she heard.

Then, what did she see?

I knock on Mila's door. I know she's home; she walked inside with Hunter and Roman only moments before. I'd been waiting for them to come back so I could talk to them in person. I no longer trust that their phones aren't bugged or some crazy shit.

"Jace?" Hunter calls out as I push the door, but it's locked.

"Yeah, it's me," I call back.

The door opens, and I see Roman's back to me in the kitchen, where he's eating something. Hunter waves for me to go in, but I can't see Mila. Not until I walk closer and see she's on the kitchen counter, and Roman's eating her face. Fuck, here we go again. It's been a week of this, nonstop. It's starting to be too much. Well, too much because I'm not a part of it. I want to eat Mila… and not just her face.

"So, the cops came to school to question me." And that was enough for them to break apart and see me standing there at last.

"Is that why you weren't at practice?" Roman asks.

I nod.

"What did they want? Why are you even being questioned?" Mila asks as she jumps to the floor on bare feet. She's wearing the same ass-hugging jeans as she did at school, but now she's added Roman's hoodie, and it makes her look so small. But incredibly sexy.

She comes to me, and I look down into her blue eyes, and my hand itches to brush her hair back behind her ear and to run my thumb over her plump lips. Fuck, I want to kiss her so badly.

"You." Her brows furrow, and I want to touch them too, to ease her worry. Would she let me? I clench my hands as she takes a step away from me before I get the chance to try. It's for the best. This isn't the right time.

"What? Me? They asked you about me? The investigation's over, I thought. It was self-defense."

I nod. "Yeah, well, they seem to be very interested in your relationship with Hunter and Roman. The Amato family. And they think I know something because we're friends. I don't know shit. But Britney Montlake seems to think you're all going to prison."

Mila gasps. Hunter wraps his arms around her as Roman paces in the kitchen. He looks to the window and the door. Fuck, what have they gotten themselves into?

"What do you mean, Britney thinks we're going to prison?" Hunter questions as he rubs a palm up and down Mila's arm. *Ugh…* it's getting to me. Watching them and wanting it to be me holding her.

I throw my hands up to stop myself from taking her into my arms and soothing her worries. "I don't know. I asked her what she'd heard, and she told me it wasn't what she heard but what she *saw*. Britney's just mad at me, and I think she's trying to start shit. Unless something did happen?"

Hunter shakes his head. "She saw nothing because *nothing* happened."

His eye twitches, and I know he's lying. I point to

him. I hate being in the dark, and this… I need to know the truth.

"I hear you all whispering, and I know about the Amato Family. You whisper loudly. So, tell me now. Are you involved with them? Are you all fucking each other? And, yes, the cops asked me that, in front of my dad."

Hunter looks to Roman behind him, and I know I'm being unfair. They have only just forgiven me, but I don't know what I'm supposed to say to the police if they come knocking again. I want to be a part of whatever's going on, like I was before I fucked it up. I want Mila to see me as more than the screwed-up asshole she forgave, but still can't trust. Pushing her for this won't win me any points with her, but I need to know.

"Fuck." Roman throws his hands up and storms over to the sofa. He flops down and cradles his head. Shit, how deep are they?

"Fuck, just tell me. So, when they come back to question me, I know what I need to hide."

"But that's the thing," Mila says. "If we tell you, you'll have to lie. The more you know, the deeper you get."

"We can't tell you without you now being involved. If something were to come out, you would be an accessory to the… crime," Hunter finishes and shakes his head at me. He lets out a deep breath, letting go of Mila and taking a few steps away from her to pace.

"Crime?" Fuck, I just didn't want to be left out. But now I'm worried this is something much bigger than I thought. Self-defense. That's not what I would call a crime. Murder… now, that's a crime.

Roman stands up abruptly, his eyes meeting mine. He says four words that I never expected.

"I killed my dad."

Well… *fuck.*

FOUR
MILA

Jace sits on the sofa, staring at Roman like he can't believe what he just said. I'm still in shock that Roman announced it like that, he hasn't said a word about it since it happened. And he just straight-up told Jace that he killed his dad.

Although, it wasn't like that; he didn't just kill him. It was in self-defense. Not a crime like Hunter said. Except, with how much we changed and covered up, that's the crime. It would make us look guilty for tampering with the crime scene and lying about who killed him.

Roman is in the armchair, zoned out, and I'm left standing here with Hunter to pick up the pieces. If the cops are snooping around, that means something didn't add up, and I have no idea what that could be. DNA, fingerprints, shit, did Roman leave a bloody fingerprint somewhere? I assumed they would believe my story enough that they wouldn't test the whole place. Why would they? It was all wrapped up, an easy, open-and-shut case.

Roman went there to get some clothes and stuff with an officer, but that's the last time any of us have been there. He didn't say much, but maybe we should have all gone with him to do it. But wouldn't that have looked suspicious? *Fuck.*

"It's okay. It's gonna be okay, Mila." Hunter takes my hand from where I was twirling and pulling on the ends of my hair. I didn't even know I was doing that.

Will it be okay?

Our entire childhood, he has said that. *Everything will be okay.* I trust Hunter when he says it. I know he will try everything to make sure it's okay. But this is bigger than us.

Much bigger.

"I don't even understand. What… why? How? Was it really self-defense?" Jace asks Roman, who doesn't move. The only indication he's heard him is a tick in his jaw at that last question.

As if Roman would have murdered his father, he deserved it, but Roman isn't that type of person. But I guess Jace is confused and just asking questions. You can't start with, "I killed my dad," then completely shut down and not expect Jace to say something dumb. But maybe Roman just needed to say it, to get it off his chest.

"Jace," I say, bringing his attention back to me. "It was self-defense. We don't want to whisper and leave you out, but we had to protect you. From the truth, the lies…

hell, all of it." I throw my hand up. "We have so many lies, I don't know what's real and what's not anymore. It's sometimes easier to live the lie than face reality."

Jace shakes his head, but before he can speak, I put my hand up to stop him.

"Look, what we say here—it stays with us. You said you would never break my trust again, and I need to believe that right now. The three of us… we're the only ones who know what really happened. About every-thing. And if it gets out, we are *all* fucked."

He nods, his big eyes reminding me of when we were kids. Innocent and trusting. This is the Jace from my past, not the asshole quarterback with a chip on his shoulder. I give a sad smile. I've missed this boy. Where has he been?

"Mila. You can trust me. You all can. If you go down, I'll go down with you." He looks at his palm, and I do the same to mine. I run my finger over the blood pact. The blood brother mark. We all carry the same scar made from the same blade. Even if it was so we would stay best friends forever, we all now belong to some-thing bigger than friendship with these marks. Trust, loyalty, love… *family.*

"There was an accident at Roman's trailer. Only, I wasn't the one who killed Damon in self-defense. Roman did, and I took the fall to protect him."

I look at Roman, and his eyes meet mine behind his hair. It's taking everything in him not to run away. I reach my hand out toward him, wanting to comfort him, wanting him to comfort me. Waiting until he opens his arms, I sit on his lap, and when he pulls me to him, I melt under his warmth.

Hugs from Roman are becoming more frequent. Anytime he lets me in, it's a huge step forward. Like now. Even when he initiates a hug, I don't touch his chest, since that will set him off. Instead, I curl my hands into myself as he hugs me to his chest.

I turn to see Jace staring at us, and Roman nuzzles his nose into my throat as he breathes me in. Jace seems surprised. He's seen us kiss. Hell, he walked in on us earlier, and I'm a little upset about that, as I'd been worked up and was hoping one of them or both would get me off. But Jace hasn't seen this side of Roman, where he freely touches me and lets me in. It's new for all of us.

Hunter clears his throat, and all attention shifts to him. He takes a seat on the edge of the coffee table and clasps his hands together, looks over to me, and nods. Hunter will tell Jace. I don't have to relive it anymore. I do that in my nightmares enough as it is. At least I don't have nightmares about being hit by that car anymore. Sometimes, I wish I didn't have to go to sleep at all.

"Damon was getting drugs from the Amato family, and he ran up a huge debt. One that Roman has been paying off by fighting. They're the ones who hit Mila on her bike and put her in the hospital. They were sending Roman a message."

Jace's eyes widen as he turns to me. I tense and close my eyes . . . I don't want him to see me like this. I feel vulnerable and I don't like it. Roman kisses my cheek, and I relax a little.

"It's the reason we've been losing games that we should have won."

Jace stands up now and looks around the room. "What do you mean, losing games?"

Hunter is struggling, but as Roman tenses beneath me, I know I need to stay here. If he gets up, a fight will likely break out.

"I'm sorry, man, for last Friday night. But if I didn't fumble…" Hunter can't say it.

I know how much it hurt him and Roman to lose the last game of the season like that. Jace didn't take it well at all, especially since he wants that college scholarship, but they needed to lose to protect us.

Jace paces now, gripping his hair and messing it up more than it was before. "Fuck." He stares at Hunter, then finds Roman's stare. "Fuck, you've been losing games because of these Amato guys, and we finished the season out losing to the Devils. Which should have been an easy win."

Shit. The team and the game mean the most to Jace. I never wanted this to happen. I feel so guilty, and I can only imagine how Hunter and Roman feel right now. It's their game too. Their team. They hurt their best friend to protect me… *us.* They love the game and the team, and they let them all down.

"But Damon's dead. I don't get why you still had to lose. Why couldn't you have told me? We could have figured out something else."

Roman's hands tighten around me as Hunter shakes his head.

"If Roman and Hunter don't lose the easy-winning games, they will come for me." I sigh. "The Amato family was placing bets on the other team… you lose, and they win the big, easy money. They don't care that Damon's dead. He used Roman to pay for his drugs. The debt doesn't just go away. It's *inherited*." Even dead, Damon is fucking with Roman.

Jace doesn't say a word as he sits on the edge of the sofa. He watches us all, and I wait as the words sink in. It's a lot to absorb, and I just hope he understands why we had no choice.

"Fuck… just, *fuck*, man." Jace stands and wraps his arms around Hunter and hugs him. *Wow.* "God, I had no idea, and blamed you for that fumble. I… *shit*. I wish I'd known. I wouldn't have said those things. I had such high hopes for this season, and it ended up being the worst season, and blamed you both. Well, and Mila.

"I'm so sorry for being an asshole. I should have known something bigger was going on. I just couldn't see it. I was angry at the world, but then I was just angry at myself for everything I did, and I couldn't get past my own damn ego."

The room grows quiet as we all nod and accept that we've all wronged each other.

"That's all of it, no more lies," Roman rumbles deeply into my hair.

I let out a deep breath. "If we are all being honest right now, I need to tell you something." I sit up, but

Roman won't let go of me. His eyes, wide, roam my face.

I smile, letting him know it's okay. "I'm okay, we're okay," I reassure him. Although, once I tell him and Hunter about the Asher thing, they might not be okay. "It's just that, Asher—" Roman grumbles deeply. He *really* doesn't like him. I have no idea why, they never talk to one another. Maybe it's a football thing.

"As I was saying… Asher. Well, he admitted he has feelings for me, and I didn't tell you."

I look over at Hunter, and he throws his hands up and lets out a groan. "I already know. The whole Garden of Eden shit. Walker told me… fuck. Asher told me himself that night."

What night? Hunter knew this whole time?

"That's why he was a dick that morning of Walker's party. I have you, you're my girl, and he was a jealous asshole."

Oh… that night. I blush at the memory. Hunter winks at me. That was an amazing night, but Asher ruined that morning.

"He said you cockblocked him and Walker from the get-go." Hunter smiles now. "I didn't tell you, because… well, it made me happy to know that you had no interest in them. Then everything happened, and to be honest, I kinda forgot."

I did that to both of them. Walker knows his place. He's a friend, and that line is very clear, even if we flirt. It's going nowhere, and I appreciate he knows that.

But Asher. God, Asher. He moved that line when he confessed his feelings, and it would be so simple if we could just keep that line straight. Only, my butterflies are making the line all wavy and messy.

"At the Halloween party, he came to tell me he just wants to be friends."

Jace snorts, and we all look at him. What's his problem? This has nothing to do with him; it's between Hunter, Roman, and me. Asher just wants to be friends now, so what does it matter... even if the word *friend* twists my stomach? That's what he wants, and it's what I need. It will make things less confusing.

"Mila, if you think he just wants to be friends, you're crazy. Hell, you probably think I just want to be your friend. I don't, to clarify, since we are all being honest. Feelings don't just go away like that. Feelings for you... they only grow stronger."

I narrow my eyes at Jace. I know feelings don't just go away, but if I say it enough, they might when it comes to Asher. It's the forbidden fruit thing; they're not genuine feelings.

Except, why do I get butterflies when I'm around him? They're the same as when I'm with Hunter, Roman, and... Jace throws his hands up.

"I want what they have. You said I gave you butterflies. So, I'm holding out hope that you will want to act on that... *soon*." He wiggles his brows at me playfully.

Ugh, I can't deny that there are still some butterflies there, only most have their wings pulled off. There's a lot of healing that needs to happen first. I know he was hurting and lashing out, but it isn't an excuse. It happened.

"Mila, you said I did," Jace continues. "Hell, I knew

I wanted to marry you when I was old enough to understand what that meant. I want what they have, even if I don't get exactly how this works. I want a piece of your heart, and I promise to give you all of mine. Please, Mila. Tell me you feel the butterflies still."

The room is silent. You could hear a pin drop with the level of quiet. No one says a thing; they're all waiting on me. Jace wiggles his brows, and I narrow my eyes at him. Mr. Ego has returned.

"Asher gives me butterflies too," I quip back, and what I just said aloud hits me too late. I tighten my lips, not wanting to say anything else.

Roman pulls me in closer to his chest, like he's trying to keep me from Asher.

Jace flops back onto the sofa and looks at Hunter, who just stares at me, his expression falling slightly, and tears prick my eyes. I didn't want to hurt Hunter. I don't know why I said that. I wasn't thinking. For a moment, I wanted to hurt Jace. I should have kept that to myself until I could tell Hunter in private. I'm now the asshole.

"Well… *fuck*," Hunter mutters as he paces.

I'm a terrible girlfriend.

"Hunter," I call to him, my voice cracking as my heart clenches in my chest. I stretch an arm out to him, and he smiles, coming to me and kissing me.

"Don't cry, babe. It's just… I guess I should have seen it coming. It makes sense. You've grown so close. He's still a dick, though."

I chuckle, and a tear rolls down my cheek. Hunter wipes it away just as Jace clears his throat.

"So, about me again." We all turn to Jace, who has a stupid grin on his face. "What? I took my shot, and it went all sad and shit. Mila, I'm happy to wait as long as you need. Just know that, if you want to kiss me, I'm not stopping you. And I'm keeping you. *Forever*."

I don't see that happening anytime soon, since I'm not over the Britney thing yet. But… I smirk. "If I kiss you first, that's the deal. You can't kiss me or try anything until I make the first move and Hunter and Roman both agree that you can be in this relationship." Jace's eyes light up and Hunter's eyes widen.

Jace agrees to my terms.

I'm gonna torture Jace with this. It'll be fun.

I wink to Hunter and give him a *sorry* smile again for not telling him about Asher and the fact that I have feelings for him too. Ugh, why is this such a mess?

Hunter nods. He's going to want to talk about Asher later, and I don't think I'm ready for that yet. I've just really admitted that to myself. I need time to process.

It's so quiet, and I don't like the tension in the room. The air feels thicker after admitting the Asher thing than it did during the whole Roman and his dad thing. Hunter gets back up and stands beside the coffee table. He looks so sexy in his plain black tee. It hugs all his ridges, and I lick my lips just thinking about what's underneath it.

He looks to his feet and then back at us, his brows pinched together. "I'm leaving Ridgecrest."

My mouth drops open. *What?*

Hunter's joking… right? He gives a small shrug, and I can tell he's serious. What does that mean? Why's he leaving? Oh shit, I think I'm really going to cry now. I pry myself from Roman and go to Hunter, wrapping my arms around his waist.

"I won't be a Rebel anymore. I'm gonna be a King."

Pulling back to see Hunter's face, I kiss him. I want him to know I love him. I just don't understand why he's leaving.

Jace stands up and yells, "What the fuck, man? What the hell is going on here? We were supposed to be Rebels until the end…" The way Jace trails off, it's clear he's really hurting.

I'm upset that Hunter didn't tell me, but there must be a reason he's been holding onto this secret. Like how I held onto my Asher one.

When did he decide to leave?

"I'm sorry. I tried everything. I did. But shit hit the fan with my dad, and, at the time, having Roman living with me was more important than being a Rebel. I was hoping Dad would change his mind, but he won't. He was letting me have until the end of the school year, but now he's changed his mind.

"I'm transferring to Lakeview Prep after Thanksgiving. It's already been arranged, and I just didn't know how to tell you. It only just changed. I thought I had till the end of summer to convince him to let me stay at Ridgecrest for my senior year, but his plans changed."

Roman stands. "What do you mean, I was more important?"

Hunter's shaking, so I hold him tighter, and he pulls me close to his chest and rocks me. Placing a kiss on my forehead, he turns to Roman. "I made a deal with my father. He said he would sign off to have you live with us for as long as you need, but only if I go to Lakeview. He never liked the fact I went to Ridgecrest. All his colleagues' kids go to Lakeview Prep or Royale Academy.

"It wasn't even something I had to think twice about. I would do it again in a heartbeat. You're my brother, Roman. I don't care about blood and all that DNA shit. You're more my family than he is. I will always choose you."

My throat is thick and tight with that declaration. Roman comes to us. I can see he's struggling with hiding his emotions too, and I reach out to him. I want him to come closer. I want to hug him and Hunter together.

Roman takes a step closer and does just that, and even I'm surprised. His arms go around the two of us. I can hear him whispering encouraging words to Hunter, thanking him and calling him his brother, as I get choked up with tears.

Hunter's not going far. A different school is nothing. It's not like being dragged away to New York. Yes, this is going to make things a little different, and I'll miss him at lunch every day. But I don't care what school he goes to. As long as Roman's safe and Hunter's mine, that's all that matters.

The front door slams shut, and we all turn to see my dad standing there in his navy polo shirt that says, "Lakeview Prep, Assistant coach." The look on his face has me straightening up.

"Dad?" What's he doing here?

I thought we were going to have dinner at Kate's place. *Shit,* I was a little—okay, a lot—distracted, and it must be later than I thought. Where's my phone? I bet he's mad at me because I'm late. He could have called Jace's parents, and they would have come to tell me.

Dad stands there looking at where I'm wedged between Hunter and Roman, and his eyes lower to where they're both touching me. Uh-oh. He's another person I need to have a talk with. He doesn't know about my relationships.

He grits out between his teeth, "Mila, we need to talk. *Alone.*"

FIVE

MILA

"I didn't do anything wrong," I sulk into the new pillow of my new house in my new bedroom. Yes, that's right, a new house, as in Kate's house, and a new bedroom, as in the guest room I've used when I stayed the night here. Now, it's filled with boxes of my stuff.

"Mila, I understand you're upset," Kate says. "I think your dad's just a little shocked. It's startling news to hear your daughter's not only dating, but dating two boys. I think it took him by surprise when Daniel called him and told him that the police were questioning students at school about it. Would have been better coming from you, I think."

I groan. I still don't get why would it matter to the cops if I'm with two guys. Doesn't make sense at all. There's a heap of different relationships out there. Why is mine so interesting suddenly? I should've told Dad, I just didn't know how. He was just starting to be okay with me and Hunter. I didn't want to push him. Now, I've fucked it all up.

I grumble, "so unfair," into the pillow.

"He wanted to move you to Lakeview with Asher and Madison, but I talked him down from that. I told him I know what teenage girls are like, and he doesn't want to see that side of you."

I roll over to look at her. She did that for me?

Kate gives me another sympathetic smile. "I know how well females can hold a grudge."

I grin. That's very true. But I can't believe Dad freaked out so much he wanted me to move schools. It wouldn't get me away from Hunter, but he doesn't know that. I can't leave Roman.

"Thank you." I sniffle. It's been a roller coaster of emotions with everything before Dad and after.

"He will come around. You won't be grounded forever; he was just taken by surprise. And he worries for you," Kate adds.

I moan back into the pillow. "Can't you talk to him again? You said you would've dated two guys if you were my age. Now I am, and I'm being punished for it. Being grounded forever is a bit harsh. I love them. They love me. It's just…"

It's just that they need me right now. With everything going on with Roman and the Amato family, he needs me. And I need them both.

Kate pats my back and sits on the bed beside me. The mattress doesn't even dip under her weight. It's a king-size, heaps of room for three, and I want to say I hate this bed because I don't want to be here, but it's so soft and the perfect size for snuggling with my boys. It's been a dream to sleep in when I've stayed here. Now it's mine to keep. If I could only get two sexy guys here to share it with me, that would be the best.

"I'll see what I can do. Your father's just worried. After everything that's happened since you've been back, he feels guilty that he hasn't been there for you as much as he should have, and he's punishing himself for that."

I snort. More like punishing me. But I sigh. It's true. All this shit happened when Dad wasn't around. I was the one telling him I was fine, knowing that everything wasn't fine. Then bad shit just seems to follow those statements.

"Mila, your father's the most amazing man. I love him very much. There's something that he didn't want to tell you when you came back home.

"I'd asked him to move in with me just before you returned. He's here almost every day, and I'm so in love with him, so it made sense for him to be here. But when he found out you were coming home, he wanted it to be the same house, same room for you.

"I thought it was a great idea for you after being away so long. That you'd get time to bond with your dad again. Him wanting to do that for you made me fall in love with him even more. But all this bad stuff is what made him decide to officially move in with me. I'm sorry that it's gone down like this. I wanted it to be special for you. Not rushed. He's just scared for you, and so am I."

She brushes my hair from my face, but I can't bring myself to look at her.

"I don't want you to feel punished, not when I'm so happy that you're here with me. I get to see you every day, my bonus daughter. I'm so happy that you're here. I love you, Mila."

Those words cause me to turn over and look up at Kate. She's smiling. Ugh… why does she have to be so nice and sweet? I rub away my tears before sitting up. I have always wanted this. Wanted a mother figure who actually gives a shit, and now that I have one, I want to kiss her son…it's so complicated.

I hug her and whisper, "Thank you."

"Look, why don't you take the day off tomorrow? It's Thursday, so maybe spend the day getting organized here. Unpack the boxes? Or not. I don't mind. Watch a movie, relax. Go for a soak in the hot tub. But promise me you will just stay here. Don't run off after your boyfriends." She winks.

My phone blew up after I told Hunter, Roman, and Jace that I'm grounded and now living here. Surprisingly, Roman was the most vocal. He thinks me staying here will protect me from Johnny and Carlo and the rest of the Amato Family. But it gives them more targets with Madison, Kate, and Asher.

Which brings me back to the messages Roman sent about Asher, and how he would squish all my butterflies for my almost-stepbrother. That made me snort out loud. He really hates Asher.

"Yeah, I'll stay home and unpack."

Kate kisses my head and lets me go. "Now, get some

sleep. It's late." She smiles and closes the bedroom door softly behind her.

I lie back down, hugging a pillow and thinking about Roman. Mmm… touching me and pinching my nipples as Hunter spreads my legs, tracing his warm tongue up the inside of my thigh. My hand moves between my legs, and I find myself wet from those thoughts. It won't take me long to get off. It will help me relax and sleep.

Fuck this. Sleep is impossible. Even though I've gotten myself off three times, I'm awake and wishing the orgasms weren't by my own hand.

I have so many thoughts running through my head, most of them about Roman and Hunter. I've been so used to them being with me all the time that I miss them, and it's only been a day. Then I've been thinking about how bad it is to miss them this much. I don't need them around me all the time. I can do things without them. But it's been us against the world, and now it's me here alone. Without them.

I pick up my phone and open the group chat between me, Roman, Jace, and Hunter. There's a new message from Jace saying he's sorry, and he should have started the conversation off with his dad telling mine about the cops. There are also a few from Cadence and Sadie after I told them that Hunter was leaving for Lakeview.

Sadie: You're not gonna change schools, right?

Cadence: Don't even think that. It might happen now that you put it out there.

Me: I'm not moving schools.

At least, with Kate on my side, I won't be. *Fuck.* I wouldn't put it past my dad to change his mind if I mess up again. I never expected to be grounded or move to Kate's house.

I can't leave Roman at Ridgecrest. He would have Jace, but it's not the same. I need him just as much as he needs me. Who would braid his hair at lunch if I'm not there? I'm getting so much better at it now. Like a real professional. I smile at the thought of the first time I did his hair for a game.

I throw the covers off me. I'm wearing my sleep tank and boy shorts. It's all I could find of my sleep clothes, which Dad packed in boxes and moved here while I was at school. I gave up looking for something else after throwing clothes everywhere and making a mess. The room's huge, so my little clothes-throwing tantrum earlier just looks like a small pile of clothes discarded in the corner of the room.

Hunter has a huge bedroom like this, but his is full of shoes. That boy has a sneaker addiction. He said they were an investment. As someone who wears the same old sneakers that I love every day, I don't know much about that. But I believed him when he didn't let me touch a pair. The look in his eyes made me back away slowly from the sneakers. Who knew they could be worth so much money?

It's three in the morning. No one will be in the kitchen if I go for something to eat. I skipped dinner in protest of my grounding like a child, and now my stomach's growling at me. It's probably part of why I can't sleep.

I open my door, and the hallway's dark and quiet. I'm on the opposite end from Dad and Kate. Thank God. I don't want to hear anything coming from their room. Madison's room is right next to me, and across from me is Asher.

I stare at his dark wooden door. I've seen him since the whole "just be friend's thing," but apart from a smile and a nod of hello, we haven't exactly talked. Not like we used to. I don't think our conversation on Halloween made anything better… it just complicated things more.

I close my door softly behind me and turn the flashlight on my phone to guide me downstairs to find something yummy. There is always cake. The best part of Kate's job is that she loves baking cakes as much as she loves running her cake supplies store. I guess it was a passion of hers and then it just all fell into place.

My passion is drawing, and I haven't done that much since I've been back. I wonder if one box has my sketch pads and pencils. Might be nice to spend the day drawing. I don't want to push Dad by going to see Hunter and Roman. I might end up at Lakeview if I did.

I open the refrigerator and the whole kitchen lights up. I see cake and take it out. It's only got enough for two, maybe three, slices left, but I'm hungry, so I take the whole plate and grab a spoon from the drawer.

The first bite of chocolate and cream hits my mouth, and I moan. Kate's a genius; this is too good. Living here isn't going to be too much of a burden once I'm not grounded anymore.

I place the plate down on the counter next to an enormous window overlooking the yard and hot tub. There's enough room for a pool out there, hell, probably three of them. But the grass is all perfect and manicured. I assume they have a gardener for that. Unless Dad mows it. Ohh, do they have someone come in to clean the house? Kate's always so busy, and the house is always clean. I've never seen anyone, but I assume they come during the day when everyone's out. Like Mom's cleaning lady; she was the sweetest. I think she might be the only thing from New York I miss.

I lean over the counter and peer at the sky. The stars are out, and it's a clear night. So pretty. Maybe I should wish upon one. Am I too old to wish for things?

I spoon a heap of cake into my mouth and moan again. God, this is amazing, and I don't care what people think. Cake shouldn't be for dessert. It's a main meal in my eyes. All that's missing is milk. That would make this the perfect meal. I pull out a tall glass and grab the milk.

It's cool and refreshing. I pour another glass and go back to eating.

I see a message light up on my phone. It's Hunter.

Hunter: I love you, babe.

Me: I love you. Come visit me tomorrow during the day. I will be here and waiting for you both.

Hunter: Babe, you know I will. Be ready for us.

I smile at that and turn my phone over, so I'm back in the dark. I hum a little tune I heard on TikTok earlier and shuffle my feet to the music playing in my head as I try to remember the dance moves.

Kate might be letting me stay home tomorrow on the promise I won't go running off after my boyfriends, but I don't need to run off. They can run here. *Loopholes.*

I dance in a circle. The tile is cold on my bare feet, but I smile and twirl with my eyes closed. I might've disappointed my dad, and the cops might be onto me. Roman still has the Amato Family after him. Hunter's dad is making him transfer schools. Jace is waiting for me to kiss him, and Asher wants to be my friend.

But in this moment, all I care about is dancing.

I spin again and open my eyes. I'm smiling until I see a figure in the doorway. My heart stutters, and I freeze.

"Asher?" My chest rises and falls rapidly from his figure standing there in the dark. Fuck, even his silhouette is attractive. I swallow the thought away.

"Sorry, didn't mean to interrupt. I'm thirsty," he says.

My heart's pounding. I place my hand to my breastbone as if I can stop it from bursting out of my chest. "You scared me," I whisper into the dark.

He drifts into the kitchen, and I follow every move. I didn't think anyone was awake, it's so late. He pauses at the fridge as he looks over at me. I can just make out his facial features in the dark room. His eyes roam my body, and I take a step back.

"Sorry, I didn't mean to," he says as he pulls open the drawer and takes out a glass, moving to fill it with cold water from the fridge. The light from it casts him in half shadow, and I can see the outline of his body as he shifts. I swallow and nod.

He's wearing nothing but a cotton pair of boxer shorts, and even those are tight. My eyes roam down over his chest, abs, the outline of his cock… *fuck.* I keep looking down, past his thighs and calf muscles. He knows he's got a hot body. Is he doing this to distract me? Make me see what I'm missing?

My nipples peak as he turns his head and looks over at me again. Fuck, this is why it's so complicated. He moved the line from being friends to the possibility of something more. He hasn't crossed it, but if we're living under the same roof, it feels inevitable.

"Huh?" He's watching me. What did he say?

He gives me a cocky grin. "I didn't mean to scare you."

Huh? Oh, oh shit. He gives me that Asher smirk, which means he knows that he's messing with my head now. Coming in here looking like that. It's working. Stupid hormones. He's going to be my stepbrother. Now Dad's moved in, and Kate loves him… and me. I can't. I just—

"You want some more milk?"

I look to my empty glass. It's so dark in here I didn't even realize it was empty.

Wait. How did he? "You were watching me?" I narrow my eyes at him.

He closes the fridge door, the milk in one hand and his glass of water in the other. The room grows small and dark again. He stands there watching me, unspeaking, and I do the same, feeling the fabric rub against my nipples at every breath I take. His eyes roam to where they peak, and he tilts his head. I arch my back a little to show him what he's doing to me as I look down his body to see what I'm doing to him. I smile.

"I didn't want to disturb your dancing." He smirks and I raise my brows. "Your ass swinging… I wanted to take a *bite* of it."

My mouth drops open just slightly. My pulse speeds up. He knows this was our game—flirt and nothing can come of it. But now he's playing dirty.

I can't do this right now, but the butterflies in my tummy tell me to run my fingers down his chest, to rub my palm over his cock. Fuck, this is *fucked*. I have two of the most amazing boyfriends in the world. And my body is going crazy for him, and my mind is throwing up warning signals at the same time. The one guy I shouldn't want, and I want him to touch me. I want to show him how wet he's making me by just standing there.

"I want—" I start, but I cut myself off as he moves closer. I take a step back, the counter pressing into my back as he draws so close. I can feel his breath fan over my face while he places the milk carton beside my empty cup. I look at it, trying to mentally cool myself down. To force myself to walk away from him.

"What do you want, Mila?" He brushes a loose strand of hair from my face as his fingers graze down my cheek then pause on my chin. He tilts my chin up.

Fuck. I close my eyes and take a deep breath. He hasn't been like this for weeks. He wasn't like this at the party. This is the Asher who took my hand and pressed it against his hard cock and told me that "girls and guys can't be friends because sex *always* gets in the way." The one who took his shirt off to give me some "porn" then did pushups and caught me watching. Flirty and confident Asher.

And the heat between us is scorching.

I press my hand against his chest, and he presses his body weight into my palm. He moves until we're just touching, my nipples grazing over his chest with every breath we both take. He slides his leg between my thighs, and I let out a small gasp as he presses up between them. My whole body is buzzing from the pressure against my clit, and I do everything in my power not to rock against him and chase that feeling. I look up at him. He licks his lips.

My breathing picks up, it's like he has entranced me. I'm the lamb, and he's the lion, and I want him to bite me. I want this; I don't want this. I need to leave; I want to stay. Why is this so hard? What happened to just wanting to be friends? To wanting everything to go back to the way it was? This is the way it was, but now there are butterflies involved.

How are we going to live together when we ended up like this on the first damn night? I need to walk away. *Hunter*, my mind screams. *Roman*. I'm hurting them by standing here.

I run my hand down Asher's chest to push him away, but the hard ridges of his abs under my fingers move with him as he grabs the base of my neck and he tilts my head. I gasp, and it echoes in the quiet room.

I have enough sense to stop. I can't do this. I reach

for the glass of water beside me and tip it over his head. Some of it lands on me, and I take the moment to really cool off and snap back to reality.

"What the—?" He takes a few steps back as the water rolls down his hair and body.

I smirk as my brain come online, *finally.* "You seemed a little *hot.*"

The corner of his mouth tips up, and his eyes sparkle.

I grab my phone and walk out of the kitchen, swaying my hips as I walk away. He groans behind me. I pause in the doorway and look back. He's holding onto the counter where I just left him, watching me over his shoulder.

"I thought you wanted to be just friends," I state.

"I lied."

Me too.

SIX

MILA

"What's he doing here?" Roman grumbles into my ear.

His hand wraps possessively around my waist as he pulls my back flush with his body. My heart skips a beat at the feeling. I look up at him, loving how tall he is compared to me. His jaw ticks, and he doesn't look down at me. His eyes are focused on Asher standing in the doorway to the living room.

"I don't know. Just ignore him. *I am*," I say loud enough for Asher to hear me. When I look over at him, he raises his brow as if he's calling my bluff. *Fuck.* I can't ignore him and then acknowledge him in the same sentence.

I haven't spoken to him since last night, and I didn't intend to see him today… at least, not during the day. He went to school, from what I assumed, but returned while I was showering and getting ready for my special visitors.

"You're grounded." Asher crosses his arms over his chest as he leans against the frame.

"You're supposed to be in school." What game does he think he's playing right now?

He chuckles.

Ugh, I need to keep my distance until I can talk to Roman and Hunter together. I need to tell them what happened last night. If I don't, it's going to weigh hard on my conscience. We've agreed that it's the three of us. Not the three of us and Asher… and Jace. As much as I want to switch off my feelings for Jace, I can't. I waited most of my life to have him be more than my friend. What's a few more months?

But Asher, he was unexpected. Never saw him coming. Okay, my feelings didn't just come out of nowhere. I thought he was hot, but then he turned out to be nice and funny and not an asshole. We became friends.

Hours and hours of harmless flirting, teasing, and sweet talking. I told him all my problems, and he listened and sometimes offered advice. Until I couldn't talk to him anymore about problems. Because he's one of them.

Everything between us grew naturally. Just like it did with Jace, Hunter and Roman. Only, I'm not a little girl anymore with little schoolgirl crushes. I'm all grown up, I know what I like, I know what I want, and… shit, why is this so hard?

Roman's extra touchy-feely today. His big hand is warm, and the way he holds me against him makes me feel so protected. Not that I need him to protect me from Asher.

"Let's go to my room." I look up at Roman, but he doesn't stop watching Asher.

I pat his hand so he can release me enough to walk, and he does so, reluctantly, but he doesn't break eye contact with Asher, and Asher doesn't seem to back down either. *Fuck*. I don't want them to fight. I pull on Roman and he moves, not wanting to let me go.

Asher watches us from the same spot he's been in since I opened the front door. I roll my eyes at the two of them. Ugh, boys. I take Roman's hand and tug him to the stairwell, hoping that Asher takes the hint and leaves us alone. One more look back at Asher, and Roman's following me up the stairs.

"When's Hunter coming?" I ask. I'd assumed they would come together, but Roman rode up on his motorcycle. He must have gotten it back from the shop. He said it was out of action, and that's why Hunter has been driving him around. But Hunter wasn't behind him in his Audi.

"Soon. He had something to do."

Well, that's not cryptic. Maybe the something he has to do involves Lakeview, and Roman won't say it out loud.

I can't believe I only have a few more weeks left with Hunter at Ridgecrest. I feel like I've only just come back, and already, he's leaving, even if it's just to another school. It just won't be the same without him. So many people are going to miss him in class and the hallways. Not just me.

I open my new bedroom door and pull on Roman to come in. But he tugs my hand and spins me into his arms. I feel a little dizzy at the sudden movement, but the wicked look on his face has me grinning.

He bends down and kisses me. I reach up but don't touch him, hoping, with how he's been lately, that I can touch his face. He takes my hand and wraps it around his neck. My eyes open in surprise. That's never happened. I break the kiss and take a little step back. Dang, I think I'm dizzy. That's when I see Asher at the top of the stairs. He has his arms crossed again, and he's leaning on the wall in a way that forces me to acknowledge his presence there. *Ugh, fucker.*

He catches my eyes and winks.

I roll my eyes. I know what he's doing. Getting in both our heads and pushing Roman, who has the shortest temper of my two boyfriend's. Plus, he knows how to fight. Asher's just asking to have his ass kicked. Roman gives off a deep grumble in his chest. It's the only warning Asher's going to get. I can feel it in the way Roman is so tense. He's very protective of me. I love it. But I don't think Asher will love having his ass handed to him.

"Roman, come show me how to beg," I purr up at him.

His head swings back to me, and his pupils dilate. I smile playfully as I pull on his tee, backing myself into the room. He stumbles in after me, and I hold back a giggle.

Glancing back out into the hallway, his deep voice is low and husky as he says, "Fuck off and leave."

He kicks the door shut with his foot, the frame rattling with a loud boom, and then it's just the two of us in the quiet room. I grin up at him. My Viking… he has a bit of a caveman in him too. *I love it.*

"Is someone a little jealous?" I tease.

His eyes narrow as he dips his head until our noses are touching. His hair is loose and wild, framing our faces like we're in a secret place. Just the two of us.

"Beg me," he rasps, his voice deep and needy, and a shiver runs through me. *Oh yes*. He doesn't break eye contact; those ocean blue eyes have me wanting to drown in them.

"Beg *me*," he repeats.

I've awakened a monster, and *I love it.*

"Kiss me." I lick my lips, not breaking eye contact.

His eyes crinkle at the edges, and I can feel his wicked grin all the way to my core, and it clenches. *Fuck.* Is it possible to orgasm just from a look? He hasn't even touched me yet.

He grabs my arms in his big hands and walks me backward without breaking eye contact. The backs of my legs hit the edge of the bed, and he pushes me gently; I fall back onto the soft bedding. I bite my lip to stop myself from telling him how hot this is and ruining the moment. I don't want this to stop. It's only just started.

I've always wondered what lurks deep inside Roman. He never gives anything away. He's slowly opened up to me, to Hunter. But I never knew this was in him. He's all dominant and growly most days, and I'm very happy to play along.

He leans over and pins me to the bedding with my wrists tightly in his grip. I lick my lips again as he studies my face. Although Roman's expression gives away nothing, I know he won't hurt me. I trust him completely.

His body hovers just above mine. I want him to feel how wet I am, how needy he's making me, so I push my hips up to get some friction. I need to be touched. But he moves back a little, and I let out a huff.

His eyes roam my face again, and I give him a sly smirk and a wink. I don't want to stop. I want him to know I'm all down for this. I need this. I need him.

"Beg me," he rumbles deeply.

I close my eyes and let out a soft moan. I think it's very possible to orgasm from just words, so I push him for more. "Kiss me," I demand, arching into him, but his grip only tightens on my wrists.

He moves swiftly, nipping at my lower lip and growls again, "Beg me, Mila."

Oh God, I'm so close. My heart is racing as I rub my thighs together. I need him to push me over the edge. I see the hungry look in his eyes, and I know what he wants… what I need.

"Eat me."

The look he gives me. *Fuck.*

"Please, Roman. *Eat me.*"

My core clenches around nothing, and I think he's about to do as I say, but he lets go of me. I almost cry out at the loss of touch, but he reaches under my dress to where I'm so wet and needy. I arch my back and spread my thighs wider as he cups my pussy in his warm palm.

"Mine," he growls as his lips crash down on mine. I gasp as his tongue finds mine, and I can feel his possessiveness in the kiss. I love when he kisses me, but this is something else. Something more. The kiss from the door at Jace's house that day he caught us with… well, our pants down, basically. This is the same kiss. Full of need, jealousy, longing.

I reach up and grab the back of his neck again, and he grunts but doesn't push me away. His palm moves against my soaked underwear, rubbing and teasing me through the thin, wet fabric. They need to be gone. I want them off and his mouth there. As the orgasm builds higher and higher, I moan.

He shifts and drags the fabric down just enough to push two fingers into me. I gasp against his mouth and pull him close as his fingers fuck me. When his thumb finds my clit, my hips buck off the bed. I grip his hair roughly, and he groans against my mouth. I smile at the sounds he's making.

This has never happened… like, at all. After the one time we had together, where I blew his world and he blew mine, we haven't had a repeat. We've only kissed and done some light groping. I thought maybe he needed more time. Not that I don't love his kisses and small touches.

This is a whole other Roman, and I'm here for it.

Oh God, I'm so here for it. I break the kiss and gasp as he rubs circles around my clit, my body reacting to every little touch. I reach for him; I want to repay the pleasure he's giving me, but he moves away and stops his assault on my clit.

I pout, and he rolls his eyes at me, then he's back, rubbing circles before lightly rolling over it. My toes curl as the orgasm builds again. Just enough to have me on the edge, so close, then he changes shit up, and I'm left hanging. He does it again—teasing me, playing my body—and I'm so close. I want to climax, but he keeps denying me, like Hunter does. *Fuck*, Hunter isn't even here, and I'm being denied. Does Roman know Hunter does this to me?

"Please," I beg and from the glint in his eye, I know I've won. That's what he's been waiting for… me to beg. *I'm begging.*

He slides down my body, my underwear is ripped from me, and my dress is bunched up around my waist as he pushes me farther onto the bed and his eyes wander to my pussy, all wet from teasing and denying me for so long.

"I'm so wet for you, Roman," I moan as I grab my breast and arch myself toward him.

A smirk plays on his upper lip as he watches me wiggle and touch myself. He runs a finger through my folds, and I moan. When he pulls his finger up to see, it's glistening with my need, and he sucks it into his mouth. *Oh God*, why is that so hot? He moans around his finger before dropping to his knees, and gripping my thighs tight, he spreads me wider. His tongue darts out, and he tastes me. He licks and sucks on my clit, and I practically bow off the bed, reaching for something to keep me here on earth.

"Holy shit." I grip his hair tightly, and I worry it will stop him.

But it only spurs him on as he sucks on my clit again and again. My knees try to trap him there as I moan his name over and over as I come. I feel as if I'm floating off the bed as I gasp for air. My body bows, and I grip his head as wave after wave of pleasure rolls through me.

The door to my room busts open, and I crash down as fast as that orgasm hit me. As I call out "Roman," Hunter's eyes meet mine. My core clenches as he watches us, grinning. Slamming the door shut, he stalks toward us. I shake a little from the aftershocks of the orgasm just as Hunter approaches the bed.

Roman doesn't look at Hunter, like he knew it would be him and not Asher busting through the door. Only, he doesn't know Asher well enough to trust he won't. He did that to me and Hunter without a care in the world. He might bust down that door at any moment just to make his presence known. Or not. With both of them here, I think Asher knows the odds are against him.

Another shiver rolls over me. Do I like the fact that I know he's out there? *Yes.* Do I like the fact that he might try to break in? Also, *yes.* I pinch my nipple, and it's like a lightning bolt, zapping me deeply. *Fuck.* I need to talk to Roman and Hunter about last night.

"I guess someone started the show without me."

I let out a small chuckle and look to Roman. His lips glisten with my orgasm. I sit up, bending over to kiss him and taste myself on his lips.

I turn to Hunter. "Roman has only just started the show."

Then Hunter does something unexpected. He runs his finger over Roman's top lip. Roman holds still, and we both watch as Hunter sucks it into his mouth and moans.

I'm frozen in place, unsure what the hell just happened? Roman watches Hunter. Their eyes meet, and my body reacts in a way I didn't know. *Shit*. I didn't know that could be a turn on.

I want to see more.

SEVEN
HUNTER

I shake my fist out. It hurts after I punched Asher in the jaw. *Fucker*. But all thoughts of him left when I walked in and saw Roman had started without me.

We'd spoken about this earlier at home, how this was gonna go down. If Roman wanted to join in, watch me or I watch him. What he wanted, what he's comfortable doing with me there. What he isn't okay with. He said he isn't comfortable having sex with me there. I respect that.

His first time should be just Mila and him. I know they haven't gone that far. She would have told me. She's been very open about what they have done, and it's not been much. She told me that she's all his firsts. I always suspected it. I might be a little mad at myself for not waiting to give her all my firsts. But I'm the type of guy who likes to study before taking the big test.

So, sex between Roman and Mila is off the table. But there's still plenty of other stuff the three of us can do. I love my one-on-one time with Mila, but I'm happy to also spend time sharing her with Roman.

We've worked out a pretty good balance so far. Roman gets more cuddles and kissing time on the sofa while she watches her creepy crime shows—I don't get her obsession with them; they're morbid and weird—and I get her all to myself in the bedroom. But he's ready for more, and I want that for him. I truly do.

Yeah, I can get jealous, but I hold that shit in. Although I want to kiss and cuddle her to serial killer shows, I just hang out on the chair alone and play on my phone and take secret photos of them.

Roman also said that he doesn't want to have sex with me. That's a great boundary; most guys I know would freak out to even say that. I didn't think about it, to be honest, so when he brought it up, I told him, "The feeling's mutual." I respect that he told me. But I did tell him there might be times when we accidentally touch each other. Not on purpose or in a sexual way… just, if we are both naked and close to Mila, things might happen to touch.

He just grunted. I took that as, "Yeah, I know."

But the shit that he said he's cool with, that blew my mind. I know he hates to be touched. He's getting better, but don't touch his torso. I'm no therapist, but I think the blows from fighting and his dad beating on him all those years has made that a no-go zone. His face is too, but sometimes, he lets Mila touch him there.

It's become more frequent since his asshole dad's death. The only bruises he has now are from the fights down at The Shed, something I'm working on stopping.

Her gentle touch will be the way for his healing. Replace all that bad shit with good memories. He deserves that.

Roman asked before we left today if I could show him how I please Mila. What she likes, how she likes to be touched, how much pressure, when to back off to tease her.

Okay, he didn't ask all that, he said "how do I make her come," then he grunted when I asked him what he specifically wanted me to show him, and I just went all in.

But fuck, walking into the room and seeing her face all flush with her orgasm and her release on Roman's lips… I wanted a taste. I just didn't expect myself to reach out and swipe my finger over his upper lip. I didn't think I would like it as much as I did as I sucked her juices and the taste of him off my finger.

Fuck. What's happening to me?

I've never fucked a chick with another guy before, but to think about it with Mila and Roman has my dick hard. It's like when he first kissed Mila against Jace's door. That affected me in a way I didn't understand at the time. It was hot, yeah, but was it hot because it was the two of them, and I love them both. Mila as my girl and Roman as my friend and brother… or is there more to it?

Between their shocked expressions and my own confusion, I realize I'm not ready to unbox whatever that is. I put that back on the shelf for another day. Before I ruin the moment, I decide to just roll with it.

"I want to watch as you suck Roman's cock deep

into your pretty little mouth, Mila. I want to watch as he begs for you to let him come, but you edge him until he loses control."

I watch as a corner of Mila's mouth rises. She loves when I talk dirty to her. Looking down at Roman, his lips are parted and his eyes wide. I guess he isn't so used to it yet. But he will be. I can see how dilated his pupils are. He's completely on board with my suggestion.

Mila sits up as Roman moves to let her stand. She turns and kisses me, swiping her tongue over my lips, and makes a sweet humming sound. I arch my brow at her, and she bites her lower lip.

"That was hot," she whispers, and I know she's talking about what happened between Roman and me just then. Not the dirty talk.

She spins around and looks at Roman, who's now standing awkwardly in front of us.

"Go to him," I whisper loud enough for him to hear. I take her waist between my fingers and gently push her toward him.

She slowly dances, her arms rising and her hips swaying to music only she can hear.

I can't stop watching as she puts on a sexy show for us. I have to bite the inside of my cheek to stop myself from grabbing that sexy ass and bringing her back to me. Reaching down to my cock, I palm it through my shorts to stop myself from touching her. *I have to share*. I can wait. My dick will love the attention once it's his turn. Until then, we get to watch the show.

Mila pulls on the hem of Roman's tee, and he lifts it

off, showing her his muscular frame. He's a big guy. He makes use of the school gym almost every day.

As she tugs the button on his jeans, his eyes find mine, and he freezes. He grabs her hand and holds it in place. I can tell he's overthinking the conversation we had earlier. Hell, did he not think about the fact we would have to be naked in the same room? I've seen the guy naked before. Not erect, though. That will be new for both of us.

I make it easy on him and shed my clothes first. Mila watches over her shoulder as I strip down and stand there naked. I take my cock in my hand, slowly pumping it up and down.

Reaching down to my discarded shorts, I pull out the condoms I brought. I wanted to make sure I had enough, just in case this turns into a long afternoon of sex.

I throw them on the nightstand and look at the bedroom door.

Fucking Asher. He was standing right outside when I walked up the stairs. I'd knocked on the front door, but no one answered, so I let myself in. When I caught him, he fled to his room, and I chuckled.

Like that would stop me. I heard Mila calling out, and that was enough for me to see red. I stormed into Asher's room; he didn't even see me coming as I slammed my fist into his jaw. He went down, his eyes looking up at me, wondering where the hell I just came from.

"You stay away from her, you hear me."

He just narrowed his eyes and stood, his hand

holding his jaw as he opened his mouth, and it clicked. I grinned. *Good.*

"It's my house." He threw his hands up. "What're you gonna do, be here all the time to make sure I'm not near her? I live here. So does she now."

I gritted my teeth. Now that they are living under the same roof. If she hadn't told me about her butterflies for him, this wouldn't even be happening. I guess my jealous side is stronger than I thought.

"If she wants to be more than my friend, I won't hold back. I can't, man, and I'm sorry for that. I've fallen for her, and it fucking hurts to be over here and not over there."

I pointed to him as I backed out of his room. "Nothing is gonna happen with her unless Roman and I agree. And we don't. So, go have a shower, jerk off, and think about how you will *never* have Mila."

I'm an asshole. His face fell, and I even felt a little bad for the guy. I liked him. He's a great guy, but now that he wants Mila, I don't like him anymore.

I wonder if he's out there now, listening. *Fucker.* Our girl is just that… *ours.*

When I look back, Roman's pants are gone, and he's gazing down at Mila, his hand on her head as she slowly drops to her knees.

Fuck. I've heard of "a grow-er not a show-er" thrown around in the locker rooms before, but Roman's cock fucking grows into a monster dick.

I'm not comparing dicks… *okay, I am.*

Mila doesn't reach for his cock. Is she waiting for me

to tell her what to do? But before I can speak, Roman rumbles deeply, "Lick my cock."

Her pink tongue traces up the underside of his length, and he lets out a deep moan that I can feel in my balls. My hand stills on my own cock as I stumble forward a little. Fuck, this is insane. I'm gonna come before she even touches me.

"Suck it," he directs her.

I watch as her small hand wraps around his heavy girth and she gives him a lazy stroke. I match it with my own, imagining it's her hand on me.

Roman's breath stutters as she wraps her lips around his cock and sucks him deep into her mouth. She uses her hand and mouth as his hand on her head grips her hair tightly. She moans as she bobs on his cock like it's a lollipop. A big, cock-sized lollipop.

Roman closes his eyes and tilts his head back, panting and groaning. His abs tighten, and I know he's close. I move to stop Mila, but she pulls back with a pop and grins up at me. I wink down at her, and she reaches for my cock, but I'm just out of reach.

"Wanna taste me?" I murmur.

She tilts her head and smirks. "Nope, I just want to taste Roman," she teases, and that does it for me.

I grab Roman's wrist where he still grips her long blonde waves and tilt her head back. She lets out a throaty chuckle, knowing what that teasing is doing to me. I love the way she looks up at me, not at my cock, as she licks her lips and opens her mouth, her tongue poking out as her eyes beg for a taste of me. She licks a bead of my pre-cum, and I stumble forward. Her eyes light up a little, knowing just how much she affects me.

"Watching you suck his cock has mine jealous," I admit.

She reaches up with her other hand and grips my cock tightly. She twists her hand as she strokes me, then her head dips, and she sucks me into her warm mouth. I stumble again, like a virgin having his cock touched for the first time. She makes me lose my mind. I reach out to stop myself from toppling and grab Roman's shoulder for balance. I realize what I just did, but it's too late to take it back.

His body tenses under my palm, and he reaches out and shoves me off and away. *Fuck.* I didn't mean to. I put both my arms up as my cock pops free of Mila's mouth. I take a stumbling step backward and give him an apologetic headshake as he breathes deeply. His nostrils flare, and it's as if he can't see me anymore.

His body's wired for a fight, and his eyes darken. I know this side of Roman. This is how he gets before a fight. And I did that to him and feel like a fucking asshole. I should have waited my turn; I shouldn't have gone to her. My impatience has fucked up this moment for all of us.

"I'm sorry. I know, I know I fucked up. *Please.*" I add the last part on a pleading whisper, hoping he can forgive me.

He closes his eyes, his hand that grips Mila's hair lets go, and she looks up. She has no idea what just happened. Why Roman's struggling. And it's all my fault.

Roman lets out a deep, rumbling breath. Mila stands up, letting go of his cock. She's watching and assessing as the scene unfolds without speaking a word. I shake my head and give her a small, sad smile. She returns the same smile back to me and nods.

Mila can help him.

She's the only one who ever could.

EIGHT
ROMAN

I take deep breaths. In and out. A roaring sound fills in my ears, the one that comes when I fight. I don't want to go to that dark place. I hate it there. I fucking hate that I'm this way. That he made me this way. Even from hell, my father still has his grips on me.

Mila is here. Hunter is here. You're safe now.

When Hunter touched me, it was like being thrown back to a place that haunts me. My mind playing tricks on me, flashbacks of the pain, the *fear*. Spiraling me to a safe place in my mind, but it's a place that was born of fear and anger. It's where I learned to fight back, and it scares me that this can happen with Mila so close to me. I don't want to hurt her.

Living like this is hell. All I want to do is cuddle and love Mila. I can barely let her touch me. I know it hurts her, that she could trigger me. Fuck, it hurts me too. It kills me.

I want all the bad shit that happened to me to go away. I want to forget all the damaged parts of me from the past and move forward, but it can't. It's like I'm stuck in limbo.

Hunter didn't mean to touch me—I know that—but some part of me still reacts to it. It's like a reflex. I've never done that before to Hunter. Never shown how bad it is to be touched. My vision clouded, and I lashed out and hit him away without even blinking. I didn't see Hunter. I just saw *him*… my father's eyes as I had so many times before. The only time he touched me was to beat me.

Mila is here. Hunter is here. You're safe now.

I closed my eyes, and like the therapist told me to when I see bad stuff, I focused on my breathing and that I'm safe. I hadn't told her much about my father, but she knew. She understands my triggers.

Focus on my breathing and the two most important people in my world—Mila and Hunter.

Opening my eyes, I look down at Mila. Her hand hovers just above my chest, and she has a small smile on her face. I know she's trying to reach out and comfort me, but right now, it feels more like pity, and I know she doesn't mean that.

Hunter clears his throat, and a cold feeling washes over me. I fear the look I will see on his face because of what I just did. But he's smiling at me.

"Your cock is going soft. Makes mine look huge, finally." And he winks.

Mila giggles and shoves Hunter away. Her hand on his chest makes me ache for the same. I want that. *Fuck.* I run my hands through my hair and turn from them. I need a few more moments. I need to stay. I need to run. I need—

"Roman, come to me," Mila calls out.

I throw my head up and look at the ceiling. I feel her move around me, close enough to touch me, but she doesn't. I hold my breath and say something that surprises not only Hunter and Mila but myself. "Touch me. My chest. My back. *Fix me*."

I keep my eyes closed. I need to do this with my eyes closed. I need to feel without knowing where it's coming from.

"Roman?" Her voice cracks.

I grunt, my arms dropping to my sides, and stand there like a statue waiting and hoping she will follow through.

At first, I feel the air shift against my bare skin as she moves around me. She can see all my scars; everything's on display to them both right now, and I stand a little taller.

Her fingers graze the inside of my palm, and I relax a little at the simple touch. I love to hold her hand. Her hands are so soft compared to my rough, calloused ones.

I feel her trace up the inside of my arm as her fingers graze over my tattoos, her light touch almost tickling, and I let out a small sigh. It feels so nice. I didn't know it would feel like this. She pauses for a moment then continues. Her fingers dance along my shoulder where Hunter just held on to only moments before, the touch setting me off.

I tell my mind this is Mila as she dances her fingertips along the back of my neck to my other shoulder. She lets out a tiny little huff, and I open my eyes, turning to see her on her tippy toes.

She grins up at me, and I smile. She tilts her head and wrinkles her nose in that cute way that's all Mila. "You realize you're really tall, right?"

A deep chuckle rumbles in my chest. She is tiny compared to me, and I love that. I love how small she is against me and in my arms. I worry she's going to stop touching me because I'm too tall for her, but she walks on the balls of her feet so she's facing me.

I can't close my eyes now. I need to see her big blue eyes observing me. Need to see her smiling as her fingers trail a line across my chest, down slowly over my abs, until she grips my semi-hard cock and gives me a firm stroke.

My eyes widen at that. I wasn't expecting her to do *that,* and my response has her giggling. But then her face grows serious, and I worry about what she's going to say. That I'm so damaged she doesn't want to be with someone like me… someone she can't even touch.

"You don't need to be fixed, Roman. That would mean you're broken, and you're not. Far from it. Never think that anything is wrong with the way you are, because we don't. You're my Roman, and I love you for who *you* are. You're all I need. You, me, Hunter."

Her other hand moves to my chest and presses over my heart. I reach up and hold it there against me. Hunter makes a sound before he moves around my unprotected back, like he did when he entered the room earlier. He does that a lot, and I never realized it until now.

Fuck, he really is one of a kind. Best friend and my blood brother.

"We want to keep playing?" he asks me. "Or watch a movie and pig out on chocolate and popcorn?"

I don't know. After I ruined the moment, how can we go back?

I look at Mila. Her hand is still gripping my cock, and she winks up at me as she squeezes it. It's growing hard again under her touch. "Up to you. I already got an orgasm. But don't overthink what just happened." She strokes me a few times, and I groan. Tilting her head to the side, she eyes my cock, then slowly draws her gaze back to mine.

"A little encouragement? Mila, you naughty minx," Hunter teases her.

I grip her shoulder and let out a deep, shuddering breath. "Play," I answer.

I want to play.

NINE
MILA

Roman picks me up and carries me to the bed. I laugh as he throws me, and I bounce a few times.

"It's playtime, baby." Hunter's wicked grin has me tingling all over.

I wait for Roman to join me, but he doesn't. He just watches and strokes his length. My hand weaves its way down my body, and I arch off the soft bedding as my fingers find my clit. I lick my lips as I play with myself. Hunter's cock flexes under my gaze, and I close my eyes and throw my head back, moaning.

They're watching me, taking their own pleasure and watching as I take mine.

The bed dips to the right as someone joins me. I don't open my eyes. I let the mystery take over as a warm hand cups my breast and then I feel a tongue roll around my nipple as they suck it into their hot mouth.

I smile and reach up, grabbing Hunter's head. He

doesn't have hair to grip on to, but I knew that it's Hunter by the way he uses his tongue.

I open my eyes and see Roman is on the bed now, stroking his cock as he watches the two of us. I reach for him, but he shakes his head. Not coming closer. I worry he still thinks he's broken, even though he said he wanted to play.

"Big guy, you wanna watch me blow our girl's mind?" Hunter smirks over at him.

I chuckle at the new nickname. *Big guy.* Roman grunts, and it takes no time for Hunter to rip open a square foil packet and roll a condom down his length.

"Let's put on the best show for our big guy. Let's watch him blow his load as I fuck your brains out."

Well, how can I say no to that? Hunter always finds my G-spot when we fuck, and with Roman watching, I know it's only going to be so much more explosive.

Hunter wastes no time. He kisses me as he moves our bodies together, and when I open my legs, he settles his weight there. He moves his hips as he sucks on my neck, kissing me lower and rocking his cock against my wet pussy. I pull my legs up, giving him more room, and he groans into my throat.

"You're so wet, so gorgeous, lying here under me." Hunter pauses to tell me.

I look into his eyes and grab his jaw with a smirk. "Fuck me, Hunter," I demand. As much as I love his dirty talk and love begging, he needs to shut the hell up and fuck me.

He grabs under my knee and pushes my leg up to my chest, and in one swift movement, he buries his cock deep within me. We both let out a throaty moan. He pauses for a moment, letting me adjust to the position, and I nod when I'm ready.

Pulling back, he slams into me again, and my whole body alights with pleasure. It's not slow and tender when it comes to Hunter. It's always hard and fast, just how I like it.

My fingers and toes tingle as he thrusts in and out over and over again. He hits my G-spot, and I claw for him. I can't speak. I gasp as the orgasm takes me by surprise. It's so fast that I don't have time to come down before he pulls out and flips me. I turn on my hands and knees, wanting to watch Roman.

As soon as my eyes meet his, Hunter slaps my ass, and Roman's eyes widen more. Is this how he thought it would be? Is this making him happy, or is he upset watching Hunter fuck me?

Hunter slams into me, hard. I groan as my back bows, his hands grip my ass cheeks, and he slams into me again. Roman's hand keeps time; every time Hunter slams into me, he strokes himself. His breathing speeds up. He's close, and I want to watch him come. I want to come with him.

I reach between my legs and rub my clit. Hunter bats my hand away and replaces it with his as he grips my hair and yanks my head back. His movements are becoming less predictable, and all I can hear in the room is his breathing, our bodies slapping together, and Roman's small grunts as he moves closer.

Roman's so close to me, I could taste him. I stick my

tongue out, and he moves until I can lick his pre-cum. I moan at the salty taste.

"She's so close, Roman. Come on her pretty little tongue as I come inside her. I'm close."

Roman's hand movement becomes jerky as his body struggles to stay close to me, and it doesn't take long before he's coming. I open my mouth, but I'm not fast enough, and rope after rope of cum lands on my chin and the bedding. Roman's whole body shivers as I lick his cock clean.

He groans, and my core clenches around Hunter. One stroke, two strokes, and Hunter comes. I tip over the edge with him, barely able to hold myself up as he flicks my clit and another orgasm washes through me and has me collapsing.

I drop to the bed as Hunter holds my hips up, pumping a few more times before pulling out, and I'm swept up into Roman's arms. He holds me to his chest. I'm covered in a fine sheen of sweat, and I give him a sexed-up smile.

"Hey," I say as I reach up to touch his nose. It's been broken so many times, it has a slight bump in the middle. It's perfect. I run my fingers down it, and he makes a funny sound before gently biting my finger between his teeth. I giggle.

"Don't bite her fingers off, Roman. I like to see them wrapped around my cock."

I shake my head and roll my eyes. Hunter comes over and sits beside us. He pushes my hair away from my face and kisses me. When he pulls away, I can see his brows furrow as he licks his lips.

"That… I didn't think about that when I did it."

I burst out laughing, and Roman tenses as he realizes what Hunter just tasted.

"It's not bad, man. But I think we can safely say, I don't like your cum."

Then Roman chuckles. It's deep and throaty, and I smile as I press myself against his warm, naked body.

This is perfect. This is everything I always wanted.

When I wake, it's to Roman kissing my forehead, and I'm in my pajamas under the blankets. Someone must have dressed me and put me to bed.

I open my mouth to protest him leaving me, but he whispers, "Asher's mom is home, so I gotta sneak out."

I nod and watch both Hunter and Roman sneak out of my room.

I curse myself falling asleep. I didn't get to tell them about Asher. I'll call them. It needs to be done sooner rather than later.

Night has fallen and it's dark outside. The only light on is the hallway light. I can't believe I slept that long. I must have needed it, or the guys wore me out. I stretch and feel some new muscle aches. Good aches, as I remember what happened today. How open and confident Roman had been.

There's a knock at the door, and I call out for whoever it is to come in. I sit up and rub the sleep from my eyes. I blink a few times, trying to see the figure at my door, but I can't make out who it is.

"Do you need some water, Mila?" It's Kate.

I sigh. "That would be amazing."

She goes into my bathroom and fixes me a glass of cool tap water. I take it from her and guzzle it down. She laughs when I finish. "Thirsty?"

I nod. "You could say that. Thank you, that feels better."

She sits on the edge of the bed, and I instantly think about where Roman missed my mouth, and now I'm worried she's sitting in his dry cum.

"Mila," she says loudly, and I look up at her. "Mila, I was trying to ask if you're feeling okay?"

I nod again. I must have missed her asking that as I tried to find Roman's little wet patch. Well, it's a dry patch now. I should have pulled the blankets down when we were all playing. Then I wouldn't have to worry about it being on top of the blankets.

"That's good. Your father was worried, but I wasn't." I look at her again. She wasn't?

"I know why you're tired, Mila. When I said you can stay home, but you couldn't go off chasing your boyfriends, I also meant they couldn't come here. Your father grounded you, and you spent the day with them. Why would you do that?"

How does she know? I look to my open doorway and see Asher standing there in the dark.

"You told her?" I call out, angry that he would do that.

But it's Kate who answers. "No, Mila. Funnily

enough, I have cameras at the house. You don't expect a woman living alone with two kids to not have cameras to watch the house all the time, do you?"

My mouth drops open. I had no idea. I suddenly feel guilty and bad. Kate has given me her trust, and at the first moment I could, I broke it.

"I'm sorry," I mutter. I feel like shit now. The day was amazing, and now I feel like I let her down.

"I gave you my trust, Mila. But now… now you have to earn it back."

"Are you going to tell my dad?" I ask.

Her shoulders slump forward, and she shakes her head. "No, this time I won't. This is your only warning. While you're grounded, you can't go to their house, and they can't come here."

Asher makes a strange sound, like a snort.

It didn't get past Kate, and she calls out, "And why were you home? You left for school, and then you were back here. The school said you felt sick… are you really sick, or is this something I have to be worried about now?"

"I wasn't feeling well," he mumbles.

"Liar," I mutter, and Kate turns her glare on me. It's scary, so I bow my head and look at my hands. *Shit.*

"I have to agree. You're a terrible liar, Asher. You're grounded too."

Asher throws his hands up and storms off.

"I love you, Mila. Goodnight."

Kate leans over and kisses my forehead before pushing the blankets up around me like a burrito. My heart breaks at the soft and tender touches. I disappointed her, but she still wants to take care of me.

"Night." My voice cracks as I try to shut down this emotion.

Well… *fuck.*

TEN

JACE

The Shed is full. I hate this fucking place. I haven't been here in so long, and now I'm back to help Roman. To help Hunter and Mila. I want this shit to be done, and I need to know how much money it's going to take to get these assholes off my friends' backs. I don't have much to my name, but I will do whatever I can to pay them off.

"Where are they?" I ask Hunter. I want to see these Amato guys, so I know what they look like. So I know what to look out for.

But they could be anywhere in the sea of faces in the building. There are people from all different walks of life here. Men in suits, some in jeans and tees. Hell, even one guy in a Hawaiian shirt. There's a mix of money and power. The guy standing next to you could be a millionaire or could have nothing to his name. This place draws in all the shady people from every walk of life.

"I'll tell you when I see them; they rarely make

themselves seen. But they texted and told Roman who he was to fight and lose to. It makes me fucking mad, but until I can get enough money to stop them, we don't have another choice."

I want to ask him why he doesn't just ask his dad. Although, after he made Hunter move schools over taking in Roman, I doubt asking him for money for Roman would have a positive result.

Plus, Roman will never let someone pay for him. How many fights? How many football games? Months? Years? It could be endless, and then where would we all be?

I considered the idea of us all leaving, moving away when we all graduate. Fuck college. I can get a job. We can be safe in another state, in another town. The four of us.

Not five. *Fuck Asher*.

I heard what he did with Mila. Fuck, would've been hard not to; I was there when she made the call to tell Hunter and Roman about her encounter in the kitchen with Asher. It makes me angry that he thinks he can just come in and expects she'll have a spot for him by her side.

He isn't one of us; he doesn't wear the blood brother scar on his palm. He hasn't been with us all these years. There's no history there. While I want to believe that matters, I know it doesn't. Not really, in the grand scheme of things.

If anything, Asher could be the perfect guy for Mila *because* she doesn't have a history with him. He would be a fresh start without all the bullshit that comes with our past.

I've been there for all the good and bad times. Like the time she said she wasn't feeling well on the way to school and threw up all over the back seat of James's car. It was gross and made me dry heave. Or when she caught me picking my nose… okay, that happened a lot.

But it's those things that have made us all so close. All our inside jokes others don't understand. She was mine first. I loved her first, and I'm going to marry her one day. I told myself that when I was ten, and I still tell myself that. Even through the ups and downs, she's gonna be mine.

I now just have to wait until she kisses me. And I have plans to make her want to do that sooner rather than later.

"There." Hunter points into the back corner of the room. "Can you see them? Blue suit with a red tie. And the other is wearing a black jacket with sunglasses."

I see them, lurking in the back just as Roman gets ready to fight his opponent. The one chosen by them, the one they've bet on to beat Roman. And he has to put on a show and lose. Meaning, he won't get the prize money. He gets nothing for this fight, other than to keep them off his back for another week.

Hunter strides to the side of the ring, where Roman is warming up. The guy Roman is fighting looks a lot like Asher, funnily enough. The face shape and hair are very similar to his. I want to take a photo, send it to Mila, and ask if Asher's at home. I snort. Of course he is. He's grounded, just like Mila. And even if he wasn't, he wouldn't leave. He gets to be alone with her. *Asshole.*

Roman pauses for a moment to watch this guy, and he says something to Hunter. I don't move closer to hear what they're saying. I haven't been here or done this like Hunter always has. Even in the past, it was usually Hunter calling me if there was an issue. Not me down here, calling him. I've been a shit friend to Roman even before Mila returned. I just hate The Shed so much. It scares me. I just never told them that.

I turn back to watch the two assholes. Carlos and Johnny. As they talk to another guy, I try to work out what they're doing. Are they making a deal? Ugh, what can I do if they are making deals? *Nothing.*

By the time I've turned back around, the fight has started. The crowd is loud, screaming and chanting. Roman takes a few swings at the guy, then gets taken down by a leg sweep. It looks real, like Roman's trying to win, but his hits aren't as powerful as they should be. He told me how he does it to keep up appearances. No one would bet on him if he looked like he was trying to lose fights; they would kick him out. He fights and wins. Then, the ones that he can win easy, he loses. This guy he's fighting has no form. Nothing. He's new here, from the looks of it.

Roman's eyes flick back to where the Amato guys are standing, and he takes a few swings at the guy and misses. Roman gets hit in the jaw hard and stumbles. He hits the guy, and his nose starts to bleed.

They don't have a blood rule here—anything goes.

Roman strikes a few more times, and the guy wavers. Shit, he better back down, or this guy is gonna drop.

Hunter yells to Roman. When Roman turns around, his eyes are dark, and he looks angry. He turns back to the guy and stalks after him. Hunter shakes his head and waves his hand to get Roman's attention. I move in closer.

"Don't, Roman. Come back to me, man."

Come back to me? What the—*Fuck.* He's zoned out. Fight and flight mode with Roman is scary. It's like Roman's not in control, and right now, we need him to be.

When Roman lunges and hits the guy in the cheek, it's as if it's in slow motion. His opponent's eyes roll into the back of his head as his body grows slack and collapses underneath him.

My heart stops.

"Fuck, fuck. Jace." Hunter turns to me, gripping my shoulders as he shakes me.

I'm stunned while I watch Roman pace around the guy as the referee is counting. Roman looks to us, and I can see the worried look on his face. Fuck, what do we do?

"Jace." Hunter shakes me again. "Get the car. Get it now and bring it round."

My hands don't even feel like my own. I look back to where Carlos and Johnny are, and I can't see them. *Fuck.* What happens when they lose a bet? Has this happened before? What do they do?

"Now!" Hunter screams, and I'm off, pushing my

way through the crowd as I reach into my pocket for my keys.

Car. Get to the car and bring it round. We will go to Hunter's house. Fuck, do they know Roman lives there? Will they go there? Oh god, I think I'm gonna throw up.

This is bad.

I stumble through the parking lot until I reach my SUV. My heart's pounding as I try to open the door. I press the button, and nothing. My hands are shaking, and I have to consciously still them. Every second is a second they're closer to Roman. As soon as the doors unlock, I jump in and close the door. My breathing is the only thing I hear in the quiet car.

I said I wanted to help, that I wanted to come down here, but how can Hunter be so calm? How's he not freaking out right now? I grip the steering wheel and start the engine. Backing out, I drive to the front door of The Shed and wait.

Every second that ticks by, every minute turning on the digital clock, and my head is screaming, "something bad is going down." There's a security guard outside, watching me. Every few moments, he shifts the weight on his feet, and I'm worried he's going to come tell me to leave. That I can't wait here.

"Come on, come on." I look down to my phone. I want to call them, but at the same time, I don't want them to stop and answer my call if they're close. I feel useless.

The passenger door clicks open, and I jump, dropping my phone onto the floor.

"Fuck, let's go." Hunter slams the door as Roman

does the same in the back. He's bleeding from a cut under his eye, and I know he didn't have that when I left to get the car.

I put the car into drive, and I floor it.

There's nothing but silence, and it's killing me. Why aren't they talking? What do we do? What's the plan? Is there a plan for this?

"What do we do now?" I finally ask, and Roman only grunts.

Of all the times to say something, now would be the perfect time. I'm running off adrenaline, and I'm checking my mirrors every two seconds to see if we're being followed.

"There's nothing we can do." Hunter replies.

"What do you mean, there's nothing we can do? Are they coming after us?"

How is Hunter so calm right now? This is a time to freak out.

"No, the debt just got bigger."

Fuck.

ELEVEN

MILA

Nothing says grounded like spending your Saturday morning sitting in your car outside a biker club.

Hunter texted me last night and told me what happened at The Shed. It's been over a week since we were together at my new house. My dad hasn't let me off my grounding, so I go to school, then come straight back home. My new home, which is something I have forgotten, driving back to my old home a few times on accident. I call that my auto mode. I start thinking about stuff, and next thing I know, I'm pulling into the driveway and realizing I made a mistake.

So, I couldn't help last night when I found out the debt just got bigger. I hated that I couldn't be there for Roman. I knew he would be beating himself up for what happened. It's not his fault, and I want him to know that. I tried to call him, but he wouldn't answer. According to Hunter, he'd locked himself in his room and wouldn't talk to him or Jace, who was thankfully there to help.

The mechanic's shop at The Sons of Death MC is open, and I can see some guys in leather cuts working on a silver sedan and a bike. I get out of my car and close the door. Taking a deep breath, I plaster on a smile as I turn toward the shop and make my way over.

I'm in my skinny jeans and a pink top, going with the power of looking sexy and cute. The questions I'm going to ask are ones I don't think they are willing to hand out to just anyone. But maybe they will be willing to blab them to me.

The smell of motor oil hits me as I approach the open roller door. An older guy with gray hair and tattoos sees me first, and he clears his throat as he stands.

Grabbing a dirty rag and wiping his hands off, he walks over to me with a grin on his face. "Well, hello, little lady. Is there something wrong with your car?"

I smile up at him and twirl my hair around my finger. "No, I was just wondering if Pinkie was around."

"Pinkie?" He scrunches his nose as he looks me up and down.

I flutter my lashes and nod. "Yeah, Pinkie. Is he here?"

I feel someone approaching before I see them. Another guy slowly comes up from behind me, and I turn, watching him. My heart starts to race.

He's young—I would say in his early twenties—with a thin build, but the definition in his arms isn't like

Roman's or Hunter's. These muscles weren't made in a gym; they've been made from hard work and lifting heavy stuff in the shop. Black tattoos cover his skin. No color at all. The one on his throat is a heap of skulls in a pile. Yeah, that's scary but his lip ring is hot at the same time.

His green eyes don't even blink as he comes closer. The way he stalks toward me makes me feel a little nervous. I now feel way underdressed.

I take a step back, and the older guy grumbles deeply, "Bones. Stop scaring the girl."

Bones stops and blinks finally. He looks me up and down and nods. What the hell does that mean?

"Go and get Pinkie," the older guy tells Bones. "Tell him he's got a girl out here looking for him."

Bones bites his lip ring and backs up a few steps, not taking his eyes from me until he turns. Fuck… why's that so scary hot? I take a deep breath and look around.

"Don't worry about Bones. Guy's got a few screws loose, but he's fairly harmless."

Well, that's not reassuring at all. I just nod and smile. He just watches me as he gets back to work, and I stand there, feeling out of place in the workshop.

Maybe this wasn't the best plan. I didn't really think it through for very long. But I need to get to the Amato family boss and ask them to give Roman a break.

The guys are still at Hunter's; they're too scared to leave. So, I thought if I could get the Amato Family address, then I'd pay them a visit and offer some money. Like ten grand to start, to get them off our backs for a bit. Yeah, it's a long shot, but it's the only thing I can think of right now. I hate how they have targeted Roman, and I need them to stop.

Only, I don't have their address, and the only people that I know, that might are The Sons of Death. Hence, why I'm here early on a Saturday morning. They know Roman here. Pinkie does, at least. They lived in the same trailer park growing up, and a bunch of them turned out to support Roman at his dad's funeral. And his football game.

"What girl? I don't know some blonde chick—" I hear a voice and turn to where Pinkie stands with Bones. He pauses and looks me up and down. His brows rise when he recognizes me. "—Mila?"

I smile. He remembers my name too. "Hey, Pinkie. I was wondering if we could talk?"

Pinkie's cute. Not drop-your-panties hot. Just cute with those dimples, and as he smiles at me, it's obvious he knows it. He walks closer, and Bones lingers behind, tilting his head at me. My heart starts to race. There's something about Bones that's scary, intimidating, and hot all at once. It makes me want to run away but slow enough for him to catch me. Ugh, he's not my type, but I want to know why he's called Bones.

Throwing his arm over my shoulder, Pinkie turns me away from the shop and walks me over to my car. He lets me go and takes a step back, removing a packet from his back pocket and lighting up a cigarette.

"Is Romeo good?" He looks around and then back to me.

"Yeah, he's okay."

He nods and takes another drag, the embers glow brightly.

"I was just wondering if you knew the Amato family?"

He pauses for a moment then gives me a puzzled look. "And why would you think that?" He tilts his head, and I think I underestimated Pinkie. His name might sound dumb, but he's not.

"I was doing some research, and I thought they lived in Ridgecrest, but I can't seem to find their address," I answer, not really answering his question.

His eyes narrow. "You don't need to know shit about them. Just stay away. They're not people you want to mess with."

Ah, so he does know of them, at least. And I already know they're not people I want to be around. It's not like we went out of our way to mess with them. They included us in their mess.

"I'm just curious, is all. So, they do live in Ridgecrest?"

He takes another drag and purses his lips, not saying a thing. I don't think he's going to tell me anything, but I keep pushing.

"All I need is a street. Or a general area will suffice. I can find the rest on my own."

Pinkie shifts his weight and glares at me. His nostrils flare as his jaw ticks. "That's why you're down here? Where's Romeo? Does he know you're down here, asking all these questions?"

I shrug. "No, he's off doing football stuff, I guess. That's all he does." I'm hoping he'll believe Roman is busy, so he doesn't go telling Roman I'm here… at least, not yet. I need a head start.

He nods slowly but watches my face intensely. "That's good. Zero has high hopes for him to go all the way—football, college scholarship, and all that stuff. So, don't be messing with that. You're good for him. Amato family is no place for you to be."

Wow. Okay, I wasn't expecting that. They want him to go all the way with football? I had no idea. I thought they wanted him to be part of their club, not go to college. I need to talk to Roman about this. About our future. Where we all see ourselves. For me, it's wherever they are. But Hunter's plans… I don't really know anymore. We all know we will be together, but where?

"Tell Romeo that I say hi. Make sure you call him that." Pinkie drops his smoke and crushes it into the dirt with his boot.

I half laugh. I've heard this nickname a few times before. Still, this sucks. I didn't come down here to chitchat with Pinkie. Although, I'm glad I learned that they want him to go to college.

But Pinkie isn't having any more talk about the Amato Family. He opens my driver's side door, and I take that as my cue to leave. Great this was pointless.

"Well, thanks for the chat," I say as I slip into my seat, defeated. I reach for the handle, but he holds onto the door, placing his chin on his arm.

"Mila. You're good. Too good for the stuff you're looking for. Leave it be. Go be with Roman. Forget the Amato family and whatever plans you have for them. Trust me. They're not worth it."

He pauses for my answer, and I nod. He takes that as agreement.

"You want a cherry sucker?" He pulls one from his pocket and hands it to me.

I chuckle. "That's very random," I reply, though I take it because I like cherry.

He laughs. "Nah, I carry them everywhere. I'm trying to quit smoking."

I look to where he holds another smoke between his fingers and shake my head.

"Yeah, I know… old habits and shit." He grins and shrugs. "See you round, Mila. Tell Romeo I say hey." He closes my door.

"Fuck," I mutter to myself. I pretend to look at my phone until he walks away.

I've Googled the Amato Family, and I've seen all the news articles. But an address? That's not something that's been disclosed. I've looked up buildings in the city they own or are known to frequent. But they're so far from Ridgecrest, I don't understand why they would come all the way here to bet on illegal fights. The Shed is over an hour's drive from the city, so the whole thing seems odd to me.

If they're this big mobster family like the news claims, then what are they doing threatening a sixteen-year-old boy to fix fights? And why are they even out here selling drugs to trailer scum like Roman's dad?

I lean my head on the headrest and close my eyes. Think, Mila. Why would they come here to the fights? Who else knows about them? The Shed. They're there every weekend. The owner of The Shed might have an address, but it isn't open during the day, and the time I was there… well, I have no desire to go back.

So, that leaves me with nothing.

Knocking sounds on my window, and I scream out, "holy shit." Almost jumping out of my skin. I duck and move away from the window only to see Bones staring down at me with those piercing green eyes.

I hold my hand to my chest as I right myself. He opens my door and I gasp. Fuck, he just opened the door. I need to lock my doors from now on.

He bends down so he's looking at me directly. "I hear you want an address?" His voice is deep and raspy.

My eyes widen as I nod.

My plan will only work if every piece falls into place. Bones, the scary hot biker gave me an address. Said it's about five miles from Ridgecrest in an upper-class neighborhood near Royale Academy. Said it's a gated community and good luck getting in.

I told him, "I don't give a shit. I'll get in there." And he smiled at me. I don't know if he smiles much but it gave me chills and not good ones.

As I walk into the house, my phone dings, and I find a new text from my group message with Roman and Hunter.

Hunter: What are you doing?
Me: Missing you.

Hunter: Send me a sexy photo.
Me: Okay, get ready for a sexy photo.

take a photo of my toe and the nice new color of nail polish on there, courtesy of Madison. It's blue with sparkles. And what I said was the truth—I am missing him. He doesn't have to know I'm busy trying to work out how to pay off the Amato family or that I'm about to ask Asher if I can borrow ten grand.

Roman: It's my favorite toe.

I laugh.

Me: It misses you too.
Me: Love you both, gonna have a nap.

'm not lying. I'm going to take a nap… eventually. Maybe tomorrow, if I'm still grounded. I've caught up with my class work, so I have nothing better to do, anyway.

Asher doesn't reply when I knock on his door. I know he's in there. I also know that Hunter punched him last week and it hasn't changed anything between us. He has made it very clear he doesn't want to be my friend, and trying to ignore my feelings for him is getting harder.

When he doesn't answer, I press my ear against the wood. He's in the shower; I can hear him singing. Fuck it. I open his door, sit on the end of his bed, and wait for him.

He opens the door to his bathroom and comes out

with wet hair. His body's damp, and the towel covering his junk sits low on his hips. He pauses when he sees me. "And what do I owe to this pleasure?" he drawls.

I cock my brow. "I need to borrow some money."

He gives me a puzzled expression as he walks into his wardrobe. When he drops his towel, I can see his white ass. He glances over his shoulder and chuckles as he slaps one of his ass cheeks.

"I didn't come in here to see that. I guess that's just a bonus. But I need ten grand. In cash. Like, right now."

He grabs his boxer shorts and steps into them before turning around. I tilt my head and he grins.

"I didn't get to see the front," I tease.

He chuckles deeply. "I'm waiting for when you're ready to do something with it, until then, you have to wait."

I grin. *Smartass*. "Well, I guess you're gonna be waiting a long time."

He pulls on a white fitted tee and then a pair of jeans. "I can wait." He winks over at me, and I roll my eyes. This isn't why I'm here.

"I need money," I repeat, reminding him why I'm in his room to begin with.

"I don't have that type of cash. We might look like we're flush, but we aren't. We get by. My college fund is all tied up with my dad. I don't even know if it's still mine. But if I had it, I would give it to you. The most I can get you is a grand."

Okay, I knew it was a long shot asking him for that much money. I asked Asher because I know his dad is well-off and maybe he had a secret cash pile some-where. Apparently not.

"You're not even going to ask what the money is for?" That's what really surprises me.

He shakes his head. "No, if you need money, it must be for something important. If you were going to tell me, you already would have. I assume it has something to do with your huge, blond boyfriend, but I'm not asking questions or judging anyone."

Well… *fuck*. That's sweet.

"I need cash, but I guess I can sell my car. They give cash, right?"

They sell cars and give cash on the same day. I swear I've seen ads on the TV like that, but I've never really paid attention. I wish I had. I needed to Google that. I grab my phone and start typing *cars for cash* when Asher sits down beside me. The bed dips a little, and I look at him.

"Walker has cash. The guy has a safe in his own bedroom. His parents are old money rich. He might lend you the cash."

My mouth drops. "Do you think he will?"

"I'll call him."

TWELVE
MILA

Walker doesn't answer, so Asher suggests we drive over to see him. I don't want to bug him at his house for money, but this is time sensitive now. Once Pinkie gives up my plan to Roman, he, Hunter, and Jace won't let me do this. And the Amato family will just keep us scared and Roman fighting. So, it needs to happen today.

"I know he's home this weekend, and he will be happy to see you," Asher says as he pulls into Walker's huge circular driveway.

I'm surprised that Asher's helping me with this, especially when it has to do with Roman. He hates him. Actually, maybe it's more that Roman hates Asher.

"Well, we're really going to surprise him when I ask to borrow ten grand." I laugh. Nothing says hello, like rocking up to a friend's door and asking him for money. I don't want to do this, but I will pay him back. I will sell my car or beg my mom for cash… no that's not gonna happen. I will get it back to him, though, one way or another. I can promise him that.

I love Walker's house. It's absolutely gorgeous and so much bigger than Asher's. It looks like it's from a movie.

We knock on the door, and Walker answers only a moment later, looking at us with a confused expression. He's not in his usually getup; he hasn't even gelled his hair. This is a whole different Walker, but he looks more real. More vulnerable and human.

"Hey, pretty lady." He winks.

Okay, same cocky attitude, that's all Walker.

"Hey, so this is random, but I came to ask to borrow ten thousand dollars from you."

Walker furrows his brows at me, and Asher steps forward.

"What Mila means to say is, she needs ten grand right now, and she'll pay it back." Asher backs me up, and I smile up at him and nod a thank you. Asher's been different since I turned up in his room today asking for money. He really wants to help me and Roman.

"Well, I know how you can pay me back, sweet cheeks." Walker's eyebrows wiggle at me.

I give him the most bored expression I possibly can. "Sweet cheeks?" *Really?* I smack Walker on the arm. Honestly, how he gets girls, I have no idea. Well, given this mansion, I can see why he gets girls. But not the right type of girls.

"Ouch, Mila. How did you know smacking me in the arm is all the pay back I need? You know I like it rough." He winks and turns around, walking back into his house.

"Come on in," he calls out behind him, and we enter his house, closing the door after us. The grand entrance into his house is as big as the lower level on my old house.

"Walker, are you coming back?" a female voice calls out.

Oh shit, did we interrupt a special something?

Asher looks at me. "That's Walker's mom," he whispers.

"Oh." Well, that makes sense. "I should go say hello."

Asher grabs my arm and shakes his head, but I wrench out of his hold. Why can't I say hello? It's rude to come into her house and not say hello.

Is she a huge snob who will take one look at me and turn her nose up at me? Maybe. But I don't care. I've never met or seen his parents before, so this is a good opportunity to go say hello and tell her how much I love her house. If she's a bitch, then so be it. I'm more curious than anything now.

I walk over to the room she's called from and peek around the open door. I can see the blonde, short hair of a woman sitting in a chair in front of a TV that's paused. They are watching *The Notebook*. I love that movie.

"Hi there, Mrs. Murphy. Walker's just grabbing me something. He will be back in a moment, but I just wanted to say how much I love your house and *The Notebook*."

When she turns around, I see Walker's eyes looking right back at me. She is pale and thin; she looks unwell, but the smile on her face tells me she's happy to see me. *Shit*, is his mom sick?

"Oh, hello there. Do come in." She pats the arm of the chair beside her.

From the look of the coffee table and the medical devices surrounding her, Walker's mom is definitely sick. Is that why I have never met her? Does he not want us to find out? He's my friend, and he should be able to talk to me about these things. If he wants to. Having a sick parent is challenging when you're so young.

My dad lost both his parents at eighteen. He told me it was so hard on him, because he couldn't go to them for advice, comfort, or just someone to talk to about a good or bad day.

"I'm Mila," I tell her as I sit.

Asher just stands awkwardly in the doorway, like he's too scared to come in. Did Walker not want us to be in here?

She turns to Asher. "Who are you?"

Fuck, he's been friends with Walker for way longer than I have, and she hasn't even met him yet. But before Asher can reply, I do it for him.

"That's Asher, my *stepbrother*. He's on the football team with Walker."

Asher rolls his eyes at me when Mrs. Murphy isn't looking, and I smirk. He hates that word, and it's the first time I have really used it. Now that I'm living at his house, he pretty much is my stepbrother.

"Ah, I have heard of you both. Mostly you, Mila. So, tell me, are you dating my son?"

My eyes widen at that. What has Walker told her? Did he tell his mom I was his girlfriend? I'm going to kill him if he did.

"Oh, don't be shocked. I just thought, with the way he talks about you, that you must be dating. Confident and beautiful. If my son doesn't want to date you, then there's something wrong with him."

Walker chooses that moment to walk into the room. He winks at me. "I've told you, Mom. You're the only girl I need. Who needs a girlfriend when I can sit here and watch sappy romance movies with you? Don't need to do that twice. Once is enough torture," he says playfully to his mom. He grins over at me, and I smile. He's sweet with his mom.

"Oh, I don't know about that, Walker. Mila's a very pretty girl." She smiles at me, and my cheeks heat a little. She's making me blush.

"Mila is awesome, talented, and smart. She's just playing hard to get. Tell her how wonderful I am so she'll want to be my girlfriend," he teases.

His mom shakes her head and laughs. "Ah, so Mila's smart, then. Too smart to fall for your sweet talking, Walker." Then she looks at me and nods. "As much as I love my son, he's right. No smart girl wants him. All he does is leave a line of heartbreak behind him. My boy's a sweet talker and a looker. I know those type of boys from back in my day. Good for one thing only."

My mouth drops open. Did she really just say that?

"Taking care of their mommas." Then she winks at

me, and oh my god. I think I'm in love with Walker's mom. She's funny as hell. I can tell where he gets his sense of humor from.

Walker nods to the door, and I stand up to leave. "Well, I better go. It's been so nice to meet you, Mrs. Murphy."

"Marta. Call me Marta."

I smile and hold my hand out to hers and shake it. She's cold, and I can tell that it took a lot out of her to talk to us as she sinks back into her chair. I want her to know how much I like her son.

"Walker's a very sweet and charming guy. One day, he will find the perfect girl for him, and she will probably punch him."

She laughs, and Walker's eyes meet mine. He looks tired, but the sound of his mom laughing makes him smile.

"You're probably right, Mila. I hope I can see the day that he does."

Now I have a lump in my throat. How do I answer that? I want to know what's wrong with her. Is she going to be okay? I really want her to see that. I do too.

As we shuffle to the front door, I see the money on the table near the front door. I pick it up and place it in my bag. I let out a deep breath. Asher's hand is on my back. It's a small touch, but it feels comforting. Like he knows I need a moment. He brushes my hair over my shoulder and whispers in my ear, "Cancer, but she has all the best doctors in the world."

My heart clenches. I feel so bad for her. She seems like the nicest person, and she needs to see Walker be punched by the girl he loves. To be at his wedding and watch her grandchildren grow up.

I can hear Walker and his mom talking in hushed whispers, then he runs out to see us at the front door. I didn't want to just leave without saying goodbye.

"Hey, I'll come with. Just give me five."

How can I say no to the guy who just gave me ten grand in cash? *Shit.*

I didn't think about this when I drove Asher over… I guess they are coming for the ride.

"W here are we going again?" Walker asks.

I look to my GPS for the millionth time. We're getting close. I never intended to bring them along, and I haven't told them where we're going yet.

"A mob boss's house." I answered truthfully.

I'm trying to make a habit of not lying anymore, and that's a good answer. He is a mob boss, and it's his house. They can stay in the car while I make my deal, because I don't want them getting involved.

"Yeah? I thought we were gonna get ice cream or some shit. But a mob boss's house sounds fun. What's his name?" Walker jokingly asks.

"Alessandro Amato."

That's what I've read in all the news articles I could find. He's some guy in his fifties. Hell, he's a silver fox, to be honest. The press likes to take a lot of photos of him, and the fact he's named as the boss to all this underground world stuff… well, he's the guy I want to talk to.

"What the fuck, Mila." Asher grabs the dash from the passenger seat and looks over at me, his eyes wide, and he looks a little pale.

"Tell me you're joking. You're messing with us, right?" Walker's moved forward now to look at my face. He's waiting for me to laugh or something.

"We can still go for ice cream after." That actually sounds nice, because I have a feeling this will be very stressful.

They both start talking over each other and don't let me answer..

"You're crazy." Asher huffs beside me.

"Are you insane?" Walker throws his hands up.

"What's the matter with you?" Asher yells.

"Is this what the money is for?" Walker points to my purse.

"Why are you giving money to a mob boss?" Asher sounds really worried.

"What did you do?" Walker asks.

Then Asher growls. "What did Roman do?"

And that's it. I slam on the brakes and stop the car. They're both wearing seatbelts, but I love the way their heads smack back against the headrests and their faces grow angrier. They knew I did that on purpose and I'm not apologizing.

I point at Walker, "you said you would give me money. And you did so without asking what it's for." I swing my eyes to Asher. "You—" I'm angry now, "you said you wouldn't judge. That you wouldn't ask questions. You knew it had something to do with him."

The car is silent as they both stare at me like I've lost my mind. I'm running off caffeine and adrenaline. Because if I don't keep going, if I don't get this over with, then it's never going to stop for Roman. *For us.*

"You both wanted to come. I'm going to visit a mob boss and give him some cash. You didn't ask. So, you can get out here. I will go do what I need to do, and I will come pick you up on the way back, and we can go for ice cream."

They both look at each other then back at me.

"No way you're kicking us out," Walker says. "I'm not letting you go see him without us."

"I'm sorry. I shouldn't have said that about Roman. But you're not going alone, Mila," Asher adds.

I relax a little. Even though I planned doing this alone, I'm glad they're coming with me. Because I want to throw up, and I have eaten nothing but a cherry sucker all day.

"Thank you," I whisper to them both.

I need them here more than I realized.

THIRTEEN
MILA

Bones wasn't joking about the gated community part. There are enormous iron gates at the end of the road, stopping me from going any farther. But the properties inside look like they're worth millions. I whistle under my breath.

This is crazy, but this is the right place. If I was a mob boss, I would have a gated community with a nice house… mansion.

"Mila, you know what you're doing, right?" Walker asks.

"Yes," I reply with as much confidence as I can. Because I have no idea what I'm doing. And I don't want him to know that.

I roll down my window to the security guard, who walks out of his box to greet us just outside the gates. Fuck, what house number is Amato's? I can see a few expansive properties from here, but I don't know which one is his. I hope they don't ask for the number to prove I know where I'm going.

"Who are you here to see?"

I sit taller in my seat. There's a heap of cameras watching me, and I swallow the lump in my throat. "Alessandro Amato." I reply in a confident manner. Like I have done this before. This is just a walk in the park, a regular afternoon for a girl to visit a mob boss.

"Your name?" he asks in a almost bored tone.

"Mila Hart." He glances in the car at the other two, and I quickly add, "Walker and Asher. But I'm the one who's here for Alessandro."

He goes back to his box to make the call. It must be on loudspeaker because I can hear the person on the other end. There's a long pause, and Asher fidgets next to me. I reach out and grab his knee, and he stops. I can't have him doing that, might give us away that we're way over our heads.

Looking out the window, I wait for my answer. Either way, I'm getting in there. I don't give a shit how. I will jump the fence if I need to. This is something I need to do for Roman. *For us.*

I'm glad I haven't eaten. I feel so nervous and sick now. I'm so close. So close to making this all be over with. No more Carlos and Johnny. No more Roman fighting, no more looking over our shoulders all the time. It's going to be taken care of today. I will end this thing.

"I don't know who that is. Send them away," I hear a male voice on the other end of the call tell the guard. *Fuck.*

No, this isn't happening. I'm getting in there. This needs to end. I can't live another day looking over our shoulder's. I'm going to face this man and he's going to accept my money and leave us alone.

I yell out, "Well, I know who you are, and I'm coming in to talk to you."

Walker makes a squeak sound behind me, and it's messing with my head. I'm trying to be strong and confident, and that voice on the other end of the speaker already frightened me, but not enough to turn around and leave. So I don't need Walker freaking out on me now.

"No, you're not," the voice responds, and the guard just glares at me.

"Well..." *Shit.* What now? "I'm gonna climb your fence and come knock on your door."

Asher's the one to gasp now, and my heart's racing a million miles a minute as the guard grabs for his holster. *Ugh, crap.* Well, there goes that plan. I don't want to get shot. That won't help anyone. Maybe I can sneak in another way?

I hear a small chuckle down the line. "I'd like to see you try, princess." The voice is smoother now. He doesn't sound like how I thought he would. He sounds younger than his photos, but it might just be the speaker.

I lean out my window and look up at the cameras, hoping he can see me on one of them, and try my best at flirting over the camera with a middle-aged man. "I bet you would," I purr.

The laugher down the line has me grinning. And he says, "Let them in."

My heart races. I did it, I got us in. One step closer to

my plan. Now I have to find the house and the man in question. Not freak out and run away like my mind keeps telling me to. Ask him to keep his thugs at bay. No more fighting for Roman, no more hitting me with their car. Give him ten grand and promise I can come up with the rest of the cash owed.

I want this to work so badly, I'll even ask my mom for money. If they agree to cash instead of the bets and fights, I will do it. I'll make the call.

The gates open, and the guard tells us it's the house at the very end. I slowly drive past all these big houses. Fancy cars in driveways. I almost stop when I see the house at the end.

"Holy shit," Asher whispers, and that's exactly what I'd been thinking. *Holy shit.*

It's insane. At least three times the size of Walkers' house, and so many windows. Huge, white columns were so elegant. It wasn't what I expected, but then, I guess, what did I expect a mob house to look like? All black?

I drive up the long circular driveway, feeling out of place with my little old Honda, next to all these sleek black BMWs. I put the brake on and turn the engine off. My fingers tingle, and I clench my fists. I can't stop now. I'm almost there.

Walker's car would have matched in here. But his is white. And a Mercedes Benz. But at least it wouldn't have stuck out like a sore thumb that my car was.

We all get out of the car and, just as Asher closes his door, a man in a suit opens the front door. My hands shake. I'm about to meet Alessandro Amato. I have only seen photos of him. I'm going to do it. I've come this far, and now that it's happening, I might be really freaking out. But I hold my bag in my hands and take the steps up to the front door, Walker and Asher behind me.

A man in a dark suit opens the door. He's similar looking to the guard at the front gate. He looks me once over, his expression unchanging.

"Mila Hart." I nod. He takes my bag and looks inside, then pats me down. Oh, well, I guess that makes sense. He does the same to Walker and Asher. The look son their faces is priceless. And if we weren't in the house of Alessandro Amato, I would have taken a photo.

"Follow me." He grunts as he turns, and we follow him inside.

The interior is just as beautiful and big as its exterior. A set of dramatic marble staircases leads to the second story, and the floors are so shiny that I worry I will slip on my ass even with my sneakers on. I'm so under-dressed to be in this house.

The man leads us down a hallway, past an enormous kitchen, and into a room full of white leather couches, a dark-haired guy is sitting back, eyeing me as we enter the room. He waves his hand, dismissing the security guard. I hear movement from the side, and another guy in a suit I didn't even see opens a door and leaves.

"I would say it's a pleasure to meet you, but I have no idea who you are or why you're here." He leans forward, his elbows on his knees. He looks me up and down with dark, piercing eyes.

Who the fuck is this? This isn't who I came here for. Am I at the wrong house? I look around the room and there are no photos, just pictures… and they look real. Not the fake type. I said Alessandro Amato, right? I'm not dreaming I said that.

I look to where the guard from the front door left. I want to call out and tell him he took us to the wrong person. A middle-aged guy with black and silver hair is what I'm looking for. And what I have in front of me is not that. It's the opposite to that. I have a young guy here… maybe eighteen with dark hair.

He's wearing in a polo and black skinny leg jeans. He knows he's attractive by the way he moves, you can tell he's sure of himself. He's attractive, and you can feel the power radiating from him.

He's got that big dick energy.

But I need to see the mob boss. Not this guy. I need the one in charge.

"Who are you?" I ask. The nerves creeping in more than I want and it's reflected in my voice.

"You came here for me, Mila Hart. So, you should know that." He cocks his brow.

I realize then, that he's the guy who'd been on the other end of the call at the guard box. This isn't Alessandro Amato middle aged mob boss. This is some guy, who's probably still in high school and trying to play the big, bad boss while the boss isn't here. His position is higher than the others around, I can tell that, but who is he?

"You're not who I'm here for." I'm confused. Is this a joke? This guy is fucking with me.

Asher moves closer to me, pressing his hand into my lower back, as Walker speaks up next. "Who the fuck are you?"

I reach out and grab Walker's hand as he takes another step closer to the guy, who just raises his brow and chuckles at us. "Mila, your boyfriend has a little bite. I like that."

He reclines on the white couch and drapes his arms along the top, making himself look bigger. More powerful.

"He's not my boyfriend."

He tilts his head to the side, and his eyes roam my body again. Heat flares all over my body and I hate I'm reacting to him like this. He knows what he's doing to work me up.

"My *boyfriends* aren't here. This is my stepbrother, Asher, and my friend Walker. And you are?"

Hopefully, by introducing him to my escorts, he'll give me his name, at least I hope so. I'm thinking Bones sent me on some kind of suicide mission. He gave me this location. He told me it was for the Amato family. But maybe it's their rivals. But then the guard at the gate would have found that odd when I asked for Alessandro Amato. He wouldn't have called this guy up if I was in the wrong place. *Would he?*

Asher places his hand on my back, and I take a deep breath. I need to calm down. This is okay. We'll work it out.

"I'm Alessandro Amato. You were going to jump over a fence for me." The corner of his lip raises.

What? The look on my face gives away my confusion and he laughs. It's deep and throaty.

"I'm assuming you were looking for my father and not me. He's not here."

Oh, my god. He has a son. I saw nothing about that while researching Alessandro. I guess I wasn't looking for a son, so I had no idea he had one who shares the same name.

I let out a deep breath. "Fuck. Do you know when he will be back?"

Alessandro looks at Walker, then back to me. "He won't see you, Mila," he says, then stands and nods his head to Walker. "You're QB1 for Lakeview?"

Walker grunts. "Yeah, I am."

"Damn, we could have used your arm over at Royale."

I look at Walker, and just like that, he starts chatting about football like this is some regular day. Then Asher pipes in, and I'm standing there, confused as all hell, while they make friends with the mobster's son.

What does he mean he won't see me? Why? I need this to be over with and without his father, I can't do it… unless.

"Fuck this." The room grows quiet, and all eyes are on me. I don't care. I'm doing this now.

I grab the ten grand out of my bag and push it against Alessandro's chest. He holds it to his chest with a confused look. I take a step back letting go of it.

"Here. This is why I'm here. I want your father to leave my boyfriends and me alone. Roman Valentine won't be fighting and losing football games anymore. I will pay off the debt that's not even his. It's his dead father's."

I poke Alessandro in his chest, and his eyes track my finger with a look that would normally send shivers down my spine, but I don't care anymore. I'm not here to talk about football. I'm here to get this debt paid.

"If you give drugs to a junkie and expect to be paid after, that's your own dumb business mistake. Not Roman's. So, if you could call your father and ask how big the debt is, I will get the rest of the cash and call this the end and part ways. We won't be seeing or receiving more texts from the assholes who hit me with their car and almost killed me."

Asher gasps and Walker stands there, a stunned expression on his face. I'm more shocked that I said it out loud, but fuck it, it's out there now. Alessandro looks to the money and back to me, his brow furrowing a little, and that angers me more.

"I have no idea what you're talking about. My father doesn't *give* drugs to junkies." Alessandro shifts his weigh and his nostrils flare.

I make a sound in the back of my throat. I'm going to fucking hit this prick. Yes, he did. At least his lackeys did. I don't give a shit what he thinks. This is all because of his father.

"The Amato family gave Damon drugs, and when he couldn't pay, they made his son, Roman—my boyfriend—take on the debt. They make him fight in an underground club called The Shed every week. They've made him lose his high school football games. Just so they could bet on them and make money to pay off the debt. Which, considering the drugs aren't what killed Damon, they didn't give him that much. So, ten grand should cover the drugs at least."

I draw in a deep shaking breath. I don't care that Asher and Walker can hear everything. This needs to be done.

"Then, last night's fight where he was supposed to lose and didn't… I don't know how much they lost on the bet, so if you can find that out for me, I will pay it off too."

The room's quiet, and Asher reaches for my hand. I take it. I'm shaking badly and the adrenaline is starting to wear off at Alessandro's silence. I don't think hitting Alessandro will make this any better. I just needed to get it all off my chest. Even if he says no.

I need to tell him, that it's fucking bullshit, and I'm done with it all. Roman needs to be free. He needs to live his life again—all of us do—and this isn't living, looking over our shoulders every five minutes. I'm done. I want him to know I'm a person. We are real people. And I'm not gonna stop until this is over.

If they want to kill us.

Just do it already.

FOURTEEN
ASHER

I can't get my head around what Mila just said. Why she needed the money.

I took her hand to let her know I'm here for her. I had no idea that the hit and run wasn't an accident, that they intentionally hit her with their car. Or the fact that Roman is tied up in all of this because of his father.

Fuck. I take a deep breath and try to work out how to get money. I need to stop these people from hurting her… hurting Roman. He isn't a bad guy. His father was, and now all this shit. Everything Mila says and does for Roman and Hunter makes sense now.

The way she acts when she's out of the house. The way Roman watches her and protects her. Even from me. He's protecting her from the Amato family.

"Mila, sit down. I need you to start again." Alessandro's scarily calm, but I don't like it.

She tries to pull away from me, but I won't let it happen. I'm not letting go of her. I lead her to the couch and take a seat in its soft buttery leather. As Mila talks to Alessandro, I pull out my phone and send Hunter a text, hoping he will read it. Because, if shit is about to go sideways here, I need back up.

Me: Mila is at the Amato house making a deal.

I can see he's read it and the ellipses come up, as if he's typing me a message, but go away. At least he knows.

Mila's phone goes off in her bag, and she pulls it out and presses the red button next to Hunter's name. Crap, she isn't taking his calls.

"So, tell me. Who said it's the Amato family?" Alessandro asks, the way he relaxes back as if this isn't a big deal gets to me. I don't like the smug prick.

"Johnny and Carlos. They're the ones who hit me with their car, beat Roman, and tell him where he needs to go. Who he needs to fight or what game he needs to lose."

She's shaking, and I want to comfort her more, but I don't think she would appreciate that. I don't know what I can and can't do with her reading into it as more than me wanting to comfort her. Even though I want nothing more than to kiss her.

"Johnny and Carlos, you say?" Alessandro sits up straighter now. He knows those names.

"Yes. They stalked my house, and now I don't live there anymore. I'm telling you it's them. They even sent me creepy flowers to let me know they're watching."

I squeeze her hand tighter. I can't believe this has been happening to her. She never said a thing. Even Roman. It's not his fault his father was a deadbeat dad and junkie. He shouldn't be paying off his debt. And now with him dead… *shit*. That's rough.

Alessandro dials something into his phone and puts it to his ear. "Can you get Johnny and Carlos for me?" He hangs up before the person on the other end can reply.

Mila stands up, shaking her head. I don't let go of her hand as I stand with her. The fuck is wrong with this guy. Why would he bring the two guys who tried to kill her into the same room with her. I want to hit the prick. Maybe knock that smug grin form his face.

"No, no, I can't let them see me. They'll kill me, Alessandro." She pleads with him. His expression's hard. Does this guy have no heart at all? I guess in his line of work you can't have a heart.

"Over my dead body," I growl. Fuck this. I try to pull her away, but Alessandro yells out for us to stop.

"Johnny and Carlos are my babysitters, more than anything else. They're hired to watch my back while I'm at school and nothing else. So, if they're the same guys you said did all this, we're going to have a problem here."

We? No, *he's* going to have a problem. My fingers flex, and I watch as Walker cracks his neck. I'm ready to fight these guys. Walker gives a small nod, letting me know he's on the same page as me.

Her phone rings again, and she looks at the number. She lets go of my hand, her eyes widening as she looks up at me. She knows what I did.

"You told them." She hisses under her breath.

I nod. They need to know where we were. I'm

worried this made everything worse. Not better, and this Alessandro prick is gonna pay for this.

As the two men—Johnny and Carlos I assume—walk into the room, they pause when they see Mila.

Fuck… we need backup now.

FIFTEEN
MILA

can see them both, but it's as if I'm no longer in my body. I'm frozen on the spot and screaming at myself to run. Get out of here. I can't believe he called them in here. Did he not hear what I said about them trying to kill me? There's no way they are gonna just let me walk out of here alive.

Johnny waves his hand over at me and says something to Carlos that I can't hear. Hell, I can't hear anyone but the rushing sound of my heartbeat in my ears. I look down at my phone again. Asher told Hunter. My phone is blowing up, Roman telling me to get out of here, Hunter asking for an address and Jace telling me to wait for them before I do anything "Mila like."

I think that time has passed, the fact I'm even here is already, "Mila like." Hell, I'm way past "Mila like" right now and into "crazy I lost my mind," stage. Asher takes the phone from my hand and types back an address for the guys to find me. Walker's saying something, but I don't register it. I feel so stupid. I shouldn't have come here. They know, Carlos and Johnny know I'm here.

Carlos grins at me, and I can't breathe. He hit me in the car. *It was him.* He looked right at me as he did it. I swallow the lump in my throat. I look to Johnny now. They beat Roman so badly the cops thought the same car had hit him.

They almost killed me and Roman.

They wanted to kill us. Why? For fun? Pleasure? Sick fucks.

I close my eyes and take a deep breath. In and out. I came here to get rid of them from our lives, need to do this. To face this fear. I can't let them win.

When I open my eyes, everyone's watching me, I can hear again. My body isn't numb and I'm shaking. But now with rage. I tilt my chin up at them.

"You tried to kill me." I spit at him.

Carlos waves his hand in a dismissive way that infuriates me even more. Like I'm nothing, and Johnny chuckles.

"We did no such thing. Who would want to kill an *angel*."

My stomach drops at the word angel coming from his mouth. Is he serious? I look at Alessandro, the way he's standing there, watching this unfold. I don't know if he believes them or me.

"You know you did. Your car was black. You hit me on my bike when I was trying to find Roman. You took him, you beat him almost to death and left him to die."

"We have never met you, or this Roman. You have

us confused, *bitch*." My mouth drops open. He didn't just call me a bitch.

"Back up a moment." Alessandro puts his hand out towards Carlos. "One."— he holds his finger up— "Don't be calling my guest a bitch. And two, it's very odd how Mila named you both, then the way you hesitated when you first saw her tells me you knew who she was the moment you came into the room."

Johnny shakes his head, but Alessandro continues. "And three, the damage on the car that had to be fixed. You said you hit a sign? Not a girl on a bike."

I almost stumble to my knees in relief, he believes me. At least enough to know they're lying.

"No, it's not like that. We don't know her. We just go down and place bets sometimes for fun. She probably saw us down there, or something and followed us back here." He shrugs. "Saw us win some money and wants a cut from us, Alessandro. You know how these trashy girls can get when they smell cash?" Johnny nods like that answer will get him out of this mess.

Alessandro's eyes darken, and even I take a step back from his expression.

"You do *not* call me Alessandro. I'm Mr. Amato to you. You have not earned the right to call me by my first name." Their faces fall immediately.

"You're here for one thing only. To watch my back at school and work for the family. But you have been off selling drugs and gambling? Betting money on some kid and trying to destroy his life? Then hitting a girl on her bike? Well, my father will hate to hear about this."

His voice is deep and calculating and sends shivers up my spine.

I would never want to cross him. Big dick energy... I think everyone in the room knows who has the power here and it's intimidating but impressive. He's so young. They have to have at least ten years on him. But he's got them scared.

Alessandro turns to me. He nods, and I try to keep cool. Carlos and Johnny say nothing in protest, and I don't know what I'm supposed to say right now.

"Can I get a copy of the text messages they sent your boyfriend. I would like the added proof for when I go to my father. Carlos is nothing, but Johnny is my father's third cousin, so he might like to see something before he decides what to do with him, at least." I slowly nod.

I can't believe this is happening. Asher texts on my phone again. Probably asking for the proof from Roman so he can show Alessandro.

"Anything else you want to add, Mila? Have they done anything else to you?" He asks. I shake my head. This has been more than enough. "Actually, I would like to know how much they earn betting on your Roman and return it to you." Alessandro adds. My eyes widen.

I shake my head. "We don't want the money, we just want to be left alone and put all of this behind us." Alessandro watches me with a calculating glare. And for a long money I watch him. Not breaking eye contact. He blinks and nods. He texts someone and looks over to the two assholes.

Three men in suits come out of nowhere. They're

quiet and scary. Carlos and Johnny start calling out that I'm lying, that I made it up as they take them away. The last thing I hear them say is they will come for me. It's like I'm in some mafia movie. It's surreal, but scary as all hell. They will come for me?

I just stand there, and the room grows quiet. Walker just stares at me like I have the answers here about what to do next. Shit, I guess we should go? That's the right move, right? I have no idea. I look at Alessandro, have I made this worse?

"They won't be coming for you, they will be… *dealt* with."

Dealt with? Don't think I want to mess around here with Alessandro any longer than I need, so best we leave before I run my mouth or say something that will get me into trouble… like "I'm gonna jump the gate and come find you," wasn't asking for trouble.

"So… we are off to go get ice-cream now. Thank you so much for having us in your home, Mr. Amato. And thank you for helping me with my problem."

I start to back out the room and grab Walker's hand as I pass him. We're all going, and now.

"Mila… I think we can agree, Alessandro, is what you call me. Especially after the grand entrance I got from you today. Was a nice distraction and a little entertaining."

I smile at that, and Walker chuckles.

"When Mila's involved, it's always entertaining." I smack his arm and he laughs again.

"Give me your number, Mila." Alessandro asks and I freeze. Why does he want my number?

"So I can get in touch with you if I have any more questions. But don't worry. Your problem will be taken care of. You won't hear or see from either of them again."

Oh, God. Sounds a little "sleeping with the fishes" type of saying. And as much as I don't want these guys around, I don't want to know about their deaths either.

I nod and take Alessandro's phone and put my number in there. I save myself as 'Mila gate jumping girl.' So, he remembers me in a good way. He looks down at it and laughs.

"I'll show you to the door." He gestures to the way we came with his hand, and we follow him.

He turns around in the foyer and gives me back the money, I almost forgot about that. I hand it over to Walker.

Alessandro nods at him and I feel like a huge weight has been lifted from my shoulders from coming here. It's done. We are free. I smile to myself. This is going to be so much better for us all going forward now.

The guard at the door nods and opens the door for us. And I can see Roman running towards the house with Hunter on his tail. What? How did they get here so fast? Alessandro moves swiftly and so does his guard.

Fuck.

"He's harmless." Asher quickly says to them both. The guard is holding his gun. And where did Alessandro get a gun from? Did he have that the whole time. *Oh, my God.*

"Roman," I tell Alessandro. I want him to know it's Roman.

"He's very protective of Mila." Walker explains.

"Like insanely protective." Asher adds.

Alessandro nods towards Roman, and I run. I didn't realize until then how much I needed him here. As I see him, I cry. This weight is so emotional, it was pinning us down and now we're free. All of us.

He crushes me to his chest, spinning me away from the house as he hugs me tight. We drop to our knees as he takes me down with him. His back to the Amato house. When I try to look over his shoulder to see where Asher and Walker are, Roman grabs my face and pulls it to his chest again. I let out a deep, shuddering breath and let him hold me. He wants to protect me. I'm going to let him do that. I need that as much as he does right now.

Hunter wraps his arms around me. And the three of us just hold each other tight. Until there's a clearing of a throat and Hunter stands.

"I'm Hunter, Mila's boyfriend." He says. He looks down at me and smiles.

"Well, one of her boyfriends, but I don't think Roman's gonna let her go right now. So let me thank you for everything. Asher kept me in the loop on our way here."

I realize then it's Alessandro, he's talking too. Jace appears to our left, and he smiles at me before looking at the others.

"I'm Jace, future husband of Mila." He almost growls. He catches my eye, "once she kisses me," and winks. I roll my eyes and he chuckles.

"Wow, Mila." Roman lets me look over his shoulder at Alessandro.

"Three guys? You have to be someone very special to have three of them wanting to share you. But I've now met you, and I can see why." Alessandro speaks and I smile.

I'm the luckiest girl.

"Four, actually. When she's ready to admit her feelings for me." Asher states. Looking down at me, nodding. I roll my eyes, but it's painfully true. And I need to do something about my feelings for him. These butterflies aren't going away. If anything they are growing stronger everyday.

Alessandro chuckles. "Do we have number five here, Walker?"

Walker bursts out laughing. "Hell, no. I love the little firecracker, but she's too much for me to handle. But I love looking at her ass in that little red—"

Asher smacks Walker in the chest, cutting off what he was just about to say. I laugh. Roman grunts and whispers into my ear.

"Asher… he's okay." I smile into his chest. *He is*. He came with me and I'm so glad he did. I need to tell him and Walker thank you for today. I don't think I could've gone through with this without them both.

I try to stand, but Roman won't let me. He cradles me in his arms and holds me close to his chest as he picks me up. He slowly turns to Alessandro, and it's then I realize Roman has a cut under his eye and a bruise. That would be from the fight last night. The last fight he will ever be in.

"Roman, I'm sorry for what's happened. I promise you they'll be taken care of."

Roman grunts and nods, and once again I have this feeling in my chest that Carlos and Johnny will no longer be breathing… just the way Alessandro's eyes twinkle a little at the words 'taken care of.' Like he can't wait to go take care of business once he's done with us here.

Alessandro, he comes across a nice guy, cocky and self-assured. But I wouldn't want to ever cross him. Thankfully, he has a sense of humor. If he hadn't… well, I don't want to think about that. I bet his dad would have shot me before I could have even touched the gates. I'm lucky I got the Alessandro Amato with a sense of humor.

There're goodbyes exchanged, and Roman carries me to my car. Hands Asher my bag as he slips us into the back seat. Asher takes my keys out and starts the car. I can see his eyes in the rear vison mirror and I give him a brief nod. Roman just handed him the keys. He trusts Asher to drive us home. I take a deep breath and let my body sink into Roman's embrace.

Everything's going to be better from now on.

We drive in silence until we are out of the gated community and on our way back to home… wherever that is.

"Ice-cream?" I ask. And they all turn to me.

"You are the most unbelievable chick I have ever met, Mila. You know how to get a heart started. Fuck, I thought I was gonna die in there or something. And here you all are, 'ice-cream' like we just went to the movies or some shit.

"You took us to a mobsters' house like it was a normal way to spend a Saturday afternoon." Walker's eyes widen and Roman holds me tighter.

I wink over at Walker and he shakes his head.

"Yeah, okay, I still want ice-cream." He turns to look out the front again before turning around and pointing his finger at me. "Just remember, I'm not number five here. I only keep you around for your fine ass and smart mouth." He winks at me.

"I told you I'm taking you to a mobsters' house. That was the plan. And don't tell me threatening to break into a mobsters' house doesn't turn you on?" I tease back. He shakes his head.

"I get turned on by girls throwing themselves at me for a night of Walker Murphy, then leaving the next day. No strings, no drama, and no chicks trying to break into a mobsters' house. If you know any like that, send them my way."

I fake gag "boring." Roman chuckles at that and I kiss him.

"Ice-cream?" I ask him and he smiles.

"Let's get ice-cream."

SIXTEEN
HUNTER

I need to keep a closer eye on Mila. I know she's wild and strong willed, it's what had me falling in love with her the first day I met her. But maybe she's a little impulsive. I can't believe she went to the Amato house. Not only that, but— "she did what?" I turn to Asher, who's standing in my living room, retelling the tale of what went down.

"She told Alessandro that if he doesn't let her in, she was gonna jump the gate and come knock on his door."

I look over at Mila, who's still in Roman's arms, but now they're on the couch. I narrow my eyes at her and she quickly looks away from me. Yeah, she's wild and strong, but she knows my thoughts about putting herself in danger. I'm gonna remind her about that later in my room when I spank her ass for being so reckless and scaring the shit out of me.

Roman growls again. He hasn't let go of her and she loves it. Because she knows I won't go over there and grab her, sling her over my shoulder and take her to my room. It would upset Roman, and he needs her right now after the scare she gave us all.

She glances back over at me and smiles. Like she knows my thoughts. I nod once, letting her know she's in trouble and she pokes her tongue out to taunt me. I clench my teeth, holding back what I want to say. Because she's pushing my buttons now. I want to hold her too, I want to protect her.

I don't like the way she scared him or me. But one positive that happened today is that all this shit with the Amato Family is over. We don't have to have to worry about that part of our lives anymore. We can move forward and I think the best way to do this is go out, have fun with our friends.

"Roman's birthday is next week. We need to celebrate." Roman looks over at me, his eyes widen. He hates parties. And he hates birthdays more. We have tried to do something special for him every year but now Mila's back, I'm hoping that will change his mind.

"Yes, let's have a party." Jace suggests and Roman shuts that down with a loud booming "no."

"I think we should just go out, have some dinner, maybe go to that arcade place in Lakeview. Challenge Roman to some games." Mila smiles as she moves back to gage Roman's expression. He nods. Well, that was easy.

"They have laser tag there, too. That would be fun, get some teams together. Have Lakeview against Ridgecrest." Asher supplies.

That's actually not a bad idea. It's not all about

Roman then, it's just a small group of us getting together and having some fun.

"So you and Walker against the four of us?" that doesn't work out fair but I'm happy to kick Lakeview's ass while I'm still a Rebel. And kick Asher's ass. even though he did good today letting me know where Mila was. Still not happy with him trying to put the move on my girl when I'm not around.

"Heard from a little firecracker you're gonna be a King soon enough, so you're with us, Hunter." Walker chuckles as he stuffs a cookie into his mouth.

I don't like that. "I want to be on Mila and Roman's team. Jace can be on your team."

Jace protests. He's been quiet since we got back. But he watches Mila and eyes off Asher. I guess he didn't enjoy hearing what he said earlier about being number four. It's not bothered Roman, which is unusual. Maybe he's starting to like the guy? Or maybe he's just too occupied with Mila to care.

I need to talk with Mila and Roman and work out what's going on between her and Asher. Or where Jace stands.

"Why don't we just draw names out of a hat and that's how we pick the teams? We can invite Grady and Emerson. And Cadence and Sadie. That makes it five for each team." Mila stands and Roman reluctantly lets go of her.

"Or we pick, and I pick you." Roman grabs her by the waist and pulls her back into his lap. My jaw ticks. I know he needs her. He doesn't have any family but us. But still… I need her too.

My mom is on a 'wellness retreat.' My dad's at the apartment in the city where he's made it very clear he's staying and not coming home while she's away. Hell, he's barely here when she is home, so that makes no difference to me. He sent mom off to help her drinking problem. I don't know how long she'll be gone for, but I know it's just me and Roman here. And I miss her.

I miss mom, even though she's drunk most of the time. I miss just having her here, even if she was in her room sleeping it off. It didn't feel lonely. Mom was just a few rooms away. But now she's off on this wellness retreat. I've spoken to dad maybe twice. I've spoken to his receptionist more than I have spoken to him all year.

I want to tell Mila. I want her hugs now. Jealously is something I haven't gotten used to just yet. And with Jace, and now Mila's feelings for Asher. Will she have enough time to hug me? My heart sinks a little at the thought. But I know she wouldn't do that. She would never leave me out.

But I don't want to tell her where mom is, I don't want to think about it. I put on a smile and nod at Roman.

"Done, it's your birthday, big guy. You get to pick Mila. The rest, we will draw out of a hat. I'll organize it all for Wednesday." It's not his actual birthday, it's Thursday.

But Thanksgiving's on Thursday. Not that it really matters. I'll try to cook something for his birthday, but if Mila's still grounded, which I suspect so after today's disappearance, then I can't even have her over here to celebrate.

It will just be Roman and me.

Everyone's relaxed after the wild day, and I have brought out some snacks and drinks. The TV's on and they're watching an old game. It's weird to have Asher in my house, but I settle on the couch, lay my head back, and close my eyes.

It's not long before I feel the tickle of hair on my face, and I don't have hair. I shave it off every week, even though Mila keeps asking for me to grow it back. I like it short. I open my eyes just a crack and see an upside down Mila looking down at me from over the back of the couch. She grins before kissing me. I reach up and hold her there so she can't get away. But she pulls back.

"I need to clean up, can I use your shower?"

I sit up and turn to her. She winks.

"You need to clean up too."

My mouth drops open a little at that statement. I look round the room. Jace is chatting to Walker about famous quarterback's. Roman's actually sleeping and snoring. That's a first. I don't think the guys slept well in weeks. Mila holds my hand and tugs me up. I look to Asher to see his reaction. He just glares where Mila holds my hand.

If he wants to be part of this… he needs to learn to keep that shit inside.

pull away from her lips, licking the taste of her from them. "Well, this isn't the way I thought my day was going to end." I cup her face in my hand and she nuzzles into it.

Her playful smirk has me cocking my brow. "This is exactly the way I wanted it to end." She giggles and I love that sound coming from her. Especially after the scare today.

"I'm not complaining, babe. Hell, this is better." I crush my lips to hers once more and she lets out a small, soft moan.

This is exactly what I need, to get out of my head about my family falling apart and take care of my beautiful girl.

She's so gorgeous as she pulls away from me, hooking her thumbs into her jeans and shimming them over her hips slowly. Like she wants to torture me. I'm too excited. I pull all my clothes off before she's even had time to take her socks off.

"Someone's excited." She looks down at my hard cock. I stroke the length of it. She watches me as she bites her lower lip.

"Anytime you're around, I'm like this. You're gorgeous and mine, Mila. I want to show you how you make me feel."

Pull her pink top over her head and expose her black lace bra. Her nipples are hard and pink through the see-through lace. I pull the cups down and expose them to me. She grabs my head as I move in to take one in my mouth.

"Oh, God." She moans. Tipping her head back as my thumb brushes over the other nipple. "Hunter," she whispers in the tiled room. It echoes around us. I smile, knowing that if anyone comes upstairs, they will hear her calling my name. I want them to know it's me that's giving her pleasure.

I flick open her bra and move to let it fall away from her. She giggles.

"Smooth move." I smirk before I turn her around and slap her ass. She jumps a little as she watches herself in the mirror. Her cheeks are flushed, and we both watch as my hand moves down her stomach and under her matching lace thong.

Her head falls to my shoulder when I find her clit. As she makes sounds that encourage me to tease her, I stroke it softly. I love hearing those sounds from her lips, but I can't leave those lips unclaimed. I swallow her moans as I increase my finger work on her clit.

Her small hands grip my forearm as she gets closer to climax. I dip two fingers into her wet heat and she bucks forward. Curses falling from her mouth as she comes around my fingers.

I pull my fingers from her, drag them up her tight stomach and swirl the wetness around her nipple. Spinning her around, I cup her breast and suck her nipple into my mouth, tasting her.

She wraps her arms around my neck as I remove her thong. I look up into her eyes and she tilts her head with a humming sound. At first, she kisses me softly. But I don't let her pull away. I take her ass cheeks in my hands and lift her as she wraps her legs around me. I like her like this, high up and looking down at me.

I pull her hair back with one hand and lick the column of her sweet throat.

She moans.

"Fuck, Hunter. I've wanted to do this since we got back to your place."

Me too.

I back her up closer to my shower and open the glass door, and turn it on without breaking the kiss.

I grab a condom from the draw I stash them in and take Mila into the shower with me. The warm water hits her back first, and she arches her head, letting the water roll down her face and hair.

I run my tongue along her neck, licking the water that runs down, and she moans, rocking her hips against me. I stumble a little as her pussy slides against my cock. A naughty grin from Mila is all I need to have her pressed against the cold tiles. My fingers wrapped around her delicate throat, devouring her mouth as I rock against her as she grips me tightly.

Her wet hair is a little darker now than her usual ash blonde, and I tug on it so I can devour her neck and collarbone next.

"Hunter, god I need your cock in me now. *Fuck me.*" her hips working to bring herself closer to climax again. I chuckle before taking her nipple in my mouth, sucking a little before giving it a little nip.

"Can't I worship you a little longer?" I tease her other nipple, rolling my tongue around and sucking before taking a little nip. And she groans.

"No more foreplay. Fuck me or I will call Roman up here to do the job." I pull her away from the tiles and spin her, slap her ass in the small space. The sound of it echoing back to me. She rocks her pussy into me again and moans. "Please, *please fuck me*."

"You can have him after. I'm gonna make you scream so loud that all the guys downstairs will hear you and wish they were the ones fucking you."

Another slap to the ass, "but—" I cup her breast, my thumb brushing over her nipple. "—you're mine now, babe." I suck her nipple into my mouth as I circle my tongue around. She moans, and I nip her again before helping her stand on the floor.

I put the foil wrapper to my teeth and rip, and she takes it before I can pull out the condom.

Smiling, I thrust my hips out, my hard cock smacking me in the belly as she giggles. I raise my brow.

"Wasn't expecting giggles. Was thinking more along the lines of *'oh Hunter, you're so big. How will I fit you in my tight little—*" she smacks her fist against my chest, and I stumble back a few steps, the cold tiles hitting my back.

"Hey," I rub my chest where she hit me. It didn't hurt but I pout my lips at her, and she shakes her head, smiling at me.

"Are you clean?" she asks, and I stand straighter at that. Why is she asking me that? Is she worried I might have something form a past lover?

"Yes, I've always used protection. I've never gone bare with anyone." She throws the condom to the floor of the shower. I watch it confused until she fists my cock, stroking me. Now I don't care.

"Me too, and I'm on birth control." I almost don't hear what she says. What is she telling me? I've never fucked without a condom before, and she wants me to do that with her... she trusts me. I trust her.

"I love you, Mila." I take her cheek in my palm and kiss her. It's gentle, but it doesn't take long for her to make her intentions known as she strokes my cock again.

"I'm kinda nervous. I won't last long." I tell her, I think more from anticipation of going bare with her.

"Don't worry, we can always try again... and again." She smiles up at me, winking.

Oh, she's asked for it now, my little minx. I spin her around and she puts her hands on the tiles without me asking her. Arching her back and her ass just so fucking perfect. *Dang.* I slap her ass again before I grip her hair and pull her head back. Her sexy smile finds me reaching with my other hand between her thighs. I find her clit and her legs almost give out with my assault on it. I thrust two fingers deep into her warm, tight core and she moans, pressing back as she fucks herself on my fingers.

"You like that?" I purr into her ear, and she hums. "You wanna come on my fingers or my cock?"

"Your cock." I pull her hair a little more and she arches her ass up even higher. Our size difference means it's a little harder for me to take her this way. But nothing's gonna stop me from making it work.

I line my cock up and thrust deep into her wet heat.

She gasps. As I groan at the pleasure. I didn't realize how much the condom took away from feeling this bliss until now. She's so slick and warm. I'm gonna come so fast like this. But as long as she does too, I don't care.

"How does my cock feel inside you *bare*." I thrust into her again. My balls tingling. I'm fucking close already.

"So, good, now shut up and fuck me *harder*."

I pull her hair a little tighter. She moans as she tries to rock back onto my cock. But I'm not having it. I need to go at my pace. I slam again and again into her tight, wet pussy. Tyring to think about anything to stop myself from coming.

I pull out of her to give me a chance to cool down and I spin her around to face me. Her arms wrap around my neck and she presses her wet, slick body against me, her tits rubbing against my chest, and I kiss her.

She surprises me by slapping my ass. I pull back and look down at her. She has a wicked grin on her face. "Little minx." I growl at her, but she knows it. And that just spurs me on more.

I grab the back of her thighs and lift her up above my cock, and she slowly sinks down onto it. We both groan at the feeling. I love this. I love her so much. She gets me and I get her.

I grab the back of her neck in my hand and she throws her head back, almost hitting the tiles. I thrust hard and her legs tremble.

"Yes, fuck Hunter." She screams.

I thrust deeper and harder, chasing my orgasm

while she chases hers. Our wet body's working with us and against us at the same time. Her nails dig into my shoulder to keep herself buried deep on my cock. I lick the water droplets from her throat up to her ear and nip on her earlobe.

"I'm so close, babe." I whisper, so fucking close, my balls tingle with release. She moans as I can feel her pussy clench around me tight. Oh fuck.

"Come for me, babe."

Her orgasm hits just as fast and as intense as mine. My thrusts erratic as I spill deep inside her. Holding her close to me as a deep, throaty growl tears through my lips.

"Fuck," I kiss her. She smiles lazily at me, her fingers tracing my lips as she kisses me.

"Fuck is right." She pants. "Hunter. That was mind blowing." She shakes her head and water droplets go everywhere.

Hell yeah, it was. I think I forgot my name and my problems with that orgasm.

"Let me wash you up, babe."

SEVENTEEN
MILA

It's been a surreal few days. I keep waiting to wake up from this dream, that I went to the house of Alessandro Amato. Met his son and made a deal with him, only for him to take care of our problem, just like that.

Only it's not a dream because he just texted me and I have no idea what to reply or do.

Mobster son: Mila. Need to talk to you and the boyfriends. When can we meet?

I swallow as I read it for a third time, then put my phone down and pace my room. What does he want? Is he trying to tell me that Carlos and Johnny are on the loose and gonna come after me? Or that they are dead? Or…

"Mila, can you come to the living room?" dad calls out from the hallway. I freeze, staring down at my phone.

"Mila?" he calls again. I turn to my closed door. *Fuck.*

"Coming, dad." I call out. I grab my phone and open my bedroom door. Asher's standing at his doorway. He gives me a small smile. I point at him.

"We need to talk." His smile grows, and I realize he might think it's about something else… something I'm still avoiding. "It's about Alessandro Amato."

"Why?" he whispers. I show him the message on my phone and he lets out a deep breath.

"Fuck," he rubs the back of his head. "I will call hunter. You go deal with what James wants."

Jogging down the stairs and to the living room, I pause at the doorway where he sits. This looks… bad. I'm worried he is gonna ground me harder than he already did, especially since he knew I left the house on Saturday.

Hell, he would put me in a straight jacket if he knew where I had been when I left. But Asher told him we both broke out to get ice-cream. And somehow that was all forgiven.

Slowly, I tiptoe into the living room, not sure what I'm going to be met with. He raises his brows at me and I shrug.

I've been following his rules. Trying hard at least, but it's Roman's birthday tomorrow and I want to go to the laser tag place today like we had all planned. I told dad about it, but at the time he was a little upset about me just sneaking out on Saturday. As much as I want to rebel against my dad, I also don't. he's the only actual parent I have left, and I don't want to disappoint him.

"Hey, dad." I say as I sit on the other side of the room. He rolls his eyes at me and I smile.

"Gosh, Mila. Just come sit over here. I want to talk."
I look down to my phone and see it's just after seven.
He should be off to work by now. I move to be closer to
him and he smiles.

"Is everything okay?" I ask and he nods, reaching
for my hands and taking them in his.

"Look, I know, being grounded sucks, but I didn't
know what else to do. The things that were happening
scared me and I did the only thing I thought would
keep you safe. But staying around the house all day
every day is also killing your spirit.

"Madison said you barley talk to her and Asher…
well, the two of you don't seem close anymore. I'm
worried I messed up the friendships you were building
with them both."

Oh, God. I don't want to tell my dad the real reason
behind Asher and me. Crap. I smile and pat his knee.

"Asher and me are cool now, we went to get ice-
cream. remember?"

He chuckles. "How can I not remember? You both
were grounded, and you both left the house for ice-
cream? Kind of seems pointless to keep you here. so…"
I bounce where I'm sitting.

"I'm un-grounding you." I squeal and wrap my
arms around his shoulders and hug him. He hugs me
back.

"Don't get excited. I don't like all the bad stuff that's
been happening to you either, so I would prefer that
Asher or one of the boys is with you at all times. Preferably Asher or Jace. They seem like a good choice
to me."

He takes a deep sigh and I squeeze his hands.

"Dad, I get it. I understand. I don't want to upset you or scare you. I just miss my boyfriend's. And I can see where your choices are going with Asher and Jace. But I need you to understand that I love Hunter and Roman. I know it's not the normal relationship that you know. But it works for us."

He holds my hands a little longer. He's been slowly getting used to the idea of me having two boyfriends.

"I get it. You're young and you have so much history with them both. I'm glad that you chose one to be your boyfriend. Sorry two." He shakes his head.

"Its gonna take a bit to get used too. My little girl is all grown up and got boyfriend's and all. But I would like to have a word to them about dating you, respecting you and treating you like the princess you are."

I chuckle. "Dad, they do already. I wouldn't have wanted to be their girl if they didn't."

"I just want to ask one question." I nod, a little worried dad is gonna do the sex talk or something. "How do they just not get jealous and fight? I know those boys and they would fight over candy when they were kids, but I could never share Kate with another man. I would want to hit him."

Well… um. This is weird. "So they both know where they stand, everything's equal. There is jealously, but we talk it out, or I can see when it's happening and we make it work."

He smiles and nods as he looks at the coffee table.

"That's very mature of you all. That's the perfect answer. Communication."

"So does this mean I can go to laser tag tonight?" He nods and I jump up. "Yes." I fist pump the air.

"But tomorrow is Thanksgiving, and I want you here for lunch. But I know it's Roman's birthday, so if he isn't having something at Hunter's, you can invite them both here and Jace. Madison and Asher will be here. We are going to Kate's parents' house for dinner." He gives a small smile.

"Are you okay? Do her parents not like you or something?" I ask. I love Kate. She is kind and warm, but I never thought about what her parents are like. Are they like my mom?

"I want to ask you," — he clears his throat and shifts on the couch — "I have been meaning to ask you for a few weeks now, and I put it off because of everything. But…" I nod, encouraging him to say it. "I want to ask Kate to be my wife. How do you feel about that?"

My mouth drops open even though I could see that was coming. It's just so exciting to hear it from my dad. He looks so scared and worried that I'm gonna say no. why would I do that? Kate makes him happy.

I smile and hug him.

"I think I know why you're scared to visit her parents." He chuckles and I hug him again. Only now I see Asher standing at the door. And I realize there is one big complication of my dad asking his mom to marry me. He really will be my stepbrother. That makes what's between us even harder and more important that we make the right decision.

If I was to date him, if he were to be mine and we broke up. How would that be? It's not like I can just stop calling him. I would see him for the holidays and stuff. *Forever.* And if it's not a nice break up. Fuck.

I close my eyes and by the time I open them, he's gone, and my phone is going off in my pocket. He must have called Hunter already.

I let out a deep breath. One thing at a time.

Let's work out what Alessandro wants, then I will work out what I want with Asher. And how to tell my dad that I want to date my stepbrother too. Pretty sure Kate will not like that.

But the heart wants what the heart wants.

Only my heart is so greedy.

EIGHTEEN
MILA

Hunter wraps his arms around me as soon as I walk over to him at school. He pulls me in close. I miss not being able to see him… but now I'm not grounded anymore thanks to dad this morning.

My hairs up in a ponytail today, and he tugs it gently. Pulling my head back so he can kiss me. I smile up at him and his face grows serious.

"And good morning to you." I poke his ribs. He lets go of my hair as I straighten.

"What do you think he wants?" he asks, getting straight to the point about Alessandro and the message. I had almost forgotten about that… *almost.* Fuck, that message can't be ignored. I still need to respond. But this morning has been… interesting.

"Don't know but, I also don't want to know." He runs his finger down my nose, and I relax under his touch.

I really don't want to hear any bad news today. I

want to think we are all safe for another day. Roman comes towards me from where he's just parked his motorcycle. He has a blue denim jacket and a white tee with jeans on today. *Holy, hell and heaven*. That's new and I think I need to tell my lady parts to stop drooling.

He stalks over and I feel like a statue, as I can't believe this Roman is the same guy from last week. This is the Roman I knew when we were kids. He is more confident, surer of himself. He grabs my hand and squeezes as a half-smile on his face. Afraid I will say something dumb while my hormones are still running wild I just blink at him.

I'm not the only one to notice Roman. A few girls turn their heads, but he doesn't notice them. He only has eyes for me. My heart races as he tips up my chin. Oh, my God, he's going to kiss me in front of everyone. My mouth parts a little and I lick my lips in anticipation.

He brushes his thumb over my lower lip and smirks. Okay, I think I need to change my underwear. Hunter hasn't let go of me yet, and I no longer see the surrounding crowd. It's just the three of us.

Roman dips down and takes my mouth with his, and I grab the back of his neck and tug on his hair a little. He lets out a little grunt before pulling away. He runs his fingers down my arm and holds my hand.

Hunter clears his throat, and the world comes rushing back. I notice the crowd around us now. Some people have gathered nearby with their phones out. Are they taking photos of us kissing? Who does that?

I hadn't been sure what would happen now that he

doesn't have to worry about Amato Family, his father and where his next meal is coming from. Would he hold my hand still, or would he kiss me in the hallways in front of everyone? I guess I have my answer now. Or maybe the text from Alessandro sparked something in Roman, because he wasn't like this yesterday.

"We need to hear him out. See what this is all about. I need to know if it's been taken care of." Hunter says. I understand that, and I want to know that everything has been taken care of. But I'm just so scared that he's going to tell me that his dad has changed his mind, that they did nothing wrong, and they will be after us again.

"We need to talk to him." Roman adds. Ugh… I knew I would be outvoted. I shake my head a little. I don't want bad news. Not after Roman just kissed me in front of the entire school… it will be the entire school by the end of the day with all the phones that were out taking photos of us.

"It'll be all good. Maybe he loves your winning personality and wants to be part of your little harem." Hunter teases. I slap him on the chest.

"I do not have a harem." I narrow my eyes at him.

"Not yet, at least. Need more than two guys to make it a harem, but happy to help there and make it official." Jace chuckles from behind Hunter. As he opens his arms to me and puckers his lips. I just shake my head. *Good try.*

"Oh my god, you shut up." I roll my eyes, but I love this. The playful banter is back. We're back. The awesome foursome. My best friends… but why do I feel like a piece is still missing? *Asher…*

"I'm just letting you know three's company, fours a crowd." Jace teases.

"With Asher, it feels like company. But with you, it feels like a crowd."

Jace just stands there. His mouth drops open, then closes again. He doesn't have a comeback for that, and it makes me laugh. Hunter and Roman laugh too.

"Well… fuck Asher." He mumbles under his breath before raking his fingers through his dark hair.

"I will." I reply just as the bell rings for the day and his mouth falls open.

First class of the day has Britney in it. It's always such fun when she's around.

"Killer," she hisses as she passes me, shoving me out of the way. I ignore her, but it's getting old and tiring. It's been long enough that she should have already got a new nickname for me by now. Maybe after she sees me kissing Roman, I will get an upgrade.

"Hi, Roman," she practically purrs at him. I freeze and so do the rest of the guys. Well… that's new. Roman ignores her and she sashays over and takes her seat. I eye her as I pass and take my seat beside Roman. Jace and Hunter take the table behind us and we turn to talk.

"So, good news. I'm not grounded anymore." Hunter grins and wiggles his brows at me, and I try to ignore that. I have a whole day of school to get through first and the day has barely started, and I already need to change my underwear.

I don't need to be all worked up, I won't be able to concentrate in class, I will be thinking of… well later.

Speaking of later. "Do we have all the teams ready for tonight?" I change the subject to the laser tag Walker has organised for us all. Said it's on him. Can't believe how nice he is to us all. He hardly knows Roman… hell, most people barely know Roman. But Walker booked out the whole arcade just for him.

Walker said he will never forget my trip to the mobsters' house. I smile at the thought. He told me, "I never felt scared." Then admitted later, he freaked out and tried to stay calm by talking football with Alessandro.

"Yes, can't wait. Gonna kick all your asses. Grady's in," Jace lets me know. Awesome. I haven't seen him much lately, but I guess having different classes and no longer living next door to him that's bound to happen.

"Awesome. What about Emerson?" Hunter nods. "Okay, and Cadence and Sadie said they were in as well. That makes…" I count on my fingers. "Ten." Perfect.

The teacher tells us to all turn around and be quiet. Ugh… I can't wait for school to be over. I'm excited about tonight, but I'm nervous about what Alessandro is going to say.

I quickly text him underneath the table to meet us at the Arcade in Ridgecrest at seven. That we're there for Roman's seventeenth birthday and if there's going to be any bad news not to come.

I watch the… on the screen and hold my breath. I don't think I can get through today if he says he won't come.

He replied, "I'll see you there."

I let out a deep breath. Okay, this is good. This isn't bad news, but I hope Hunter is wrong in saying he wants to be part of my harem. *I don't have a harem.* I have no interest in dating the guy and I sense he isn't the sharing type.

⊲🏈⊳ ⊲🏈⊳ ⊲🏈⊳

"What do you mean, you can't come anymore?" I ask Sadie as I stuff another French fry in my mouth. I need her there tonight. I haven't seen her very much, and I really wanted her to be there so we could hang out. She changed her hair to pink on Monday and I love it. Not that purple wasn't rocking.

"I'm sorry my mom is making me do this stupid family stuffing recipe. She told me I can't go. Stupid stuffing recipe. I don't even want Turkey. I want to come with you all." She sighs. Picking up a fry, she drops it back on the tray.

I wish her mum didn't want her to make Turkey stuffing, but at the same time it's nice that her mom wants her to do that with her. A family recipe. My mom never did that with me. I don't think she's ever cooked a day in her life. Makes me wonder what she's up to right now? Probably turned my room into a nursery and stocked it with the most expensive baby stuff. I bet Malcolm's *super* excited to be an old dad.

"I can still come, though. But can you pick me up? I've been having car trouble and my dad said he will look at it tomorrow when he's off work. But I can't make it if I don't have a lift." I smile over at Cadence and bump her shoulder with mine.

"Of course, I'm over in Lakeview, but I'm sure I can swing around, or I could at least ask Jace or Emerson to come get you." Her eyes widen at his name, and I poke her.

"Is there something you're not telling me here? Or have you and Em—" her hand flies across to cover my mouth and my eyes widen. Oh, something happened.

"Nothing happened." She whispers. She lets go of my mouth and I smile.

"But you want something to happen?" She shakes her head, and her cheeks grow red as her hair and Sadie giggles.

"Oh yeah, she wants something to happen." She wiggles her brows.

"Shut up," Cadence hisses under her breath. I grin. She shakes her head at me and points.

"You told me to stay away from him, but…"

"I need to know what happened." she shrugs and sighs.

"I'm not blind. I'm too smart to hook up with him. But I also have only one chance in high school to hook up with a football player. I guess you could say it's on my bucket list. I don't want to leave here and regret not knowing how he kisses."

"And leaving with your V card. Don't tell me you're going to give him your virginity, Cadence?" Sadie asks and my mouth drops open at that. I shake my head.

"I can tell you from experience that's not who you want to give that to. Seen it in movies, about waiting for the right person. Always thought that was a crock of shit. But now I wish I had. Roman waited for me, he gave me all his firsts. I had nothing left to give him in return, and I wish I did.

"But Emerson… he's a fuck boy. If the rumours are true, he's good at what he gives. But that's it. He fucks and leaves. I don't want that for you. I want you to have better than that for your first time."

"Back up, Roman waited for you? And you have no firsts? None at all? Like as in you've done anal," Sadie whispers the last part, and I cough and laugh at the same time.

"Okay, that's the first I've got left, but Roman's cock is not going anywhere near there. He's huge."

They both try to hold in the giggles, but it doesn't work and we all end up laughing together.

"Mila, thanks. And I get it. My mom tells me to wait for the right boy. Only sometimes… I think Emerson is the right boy."

I nod. It's up to her if she wants to lose her virginity to him. If she does, I will make sure that he treats her very well or I will kill him. And I will support her in that as best I can as her friend.

The bell rings and we all groan.

"Okay, I will see you tonight Cadence. Sadie, say hi to your mom for me."

I quickly text Hunter to let him know Sadie can't make it anymore. Who can we ask at late notice to come play laser tag with us?

When Walker said that he hired the arcade, I assumed he meant that part of the venue with the laser tag and seated area. But he hired the whole venue, including all the gaming machines and a ball pit. I haven't been to this place in years. Hell, since we were kids. We would come here and all jump in the ball pit and throw the balls at each other's heads.

Yeah, we weren't very mature. But those balls hurt when they hit your face. I always played up I was injured and when they stopped, I would hurl a ball right at their nose. Lucky for them, I wasn't the best aim. But we would get kicked out more often than not. I smile at the memory. I loved those days.

There's pizza and ribs, and Walker smuggled beer for everyone to celebrate. I turn my nose up at it. I don't really like beer. It's not my thing, but I grab a bottle just to join in with everyone.

Emerson's talking to Cadence. I love the way she twirls her hair as she flirts back with him. They'd make a cute couple if Emerson wasn't such a player. They're both great people, different from each other, but I think that works. She's level-headed and smart. She's confident in her own way, she's happy in her own skin.

Okay, normally she is, but right now she seems a little insecure talking to him.

But the thing about Emerson is, I might not know him super well now. But he's just as insecure as she is. Aren't we all? He was this cute nerdy kid in elementary school. So, he knows what that feels like, to not be the most popular, or the strongest, or even the best football player.

I can see him flirting with her, but his usual pickup lines aren't working. He actually has to work to get Cadence. She isn't the usual cheerleader throwing herself at him.

"What time did you say our special friend is arriving, Mila?" Walker asks from beside me, I almost jump. I'd been so focused on the two lovebirds over there. I didn't even see him approach me. I put my hand to my chest. I'd almost forgot Alessandro's coming.

"Ah, seven. Why?" I look at my phone and it's almost that time now.

"Just I saw a car pull up front and I think he's waiting for you."

I look to the front doors of the building and sure enough there's Alessandro. He tips his head up in greeting and points to the locked door.

I see then he has three men with him in suits. He's wearing dark jeans and a black polo. He must really like polos? reminds me of my dad and his love of polos.

I walk over with Walker. Roman sees where I'm going and jogs over. Walker opens the door to let Alessandro in. One man in a suit steps inside with him and I take a step back. The other two stand guard at the door as the one inside locks it and stands behind Alessandro.

At least they don't look like Johnny and Carlos, and I'm glad. But why's he here? To tell us they are now dead? I don't think I want to know that part. As much as I love my true crime, I don't want to be an episode of it.

"Hello firecracker, breakdown any gates lately?" I roll my eyes at him, and he chuckles.

"Happy birthday Roman." Alessandro holds out a small green box to Roman and Roman hesitates before taking it from him. I didn't expect him to bring Roman a gift, and from the look on his face, neither did Roman.

"Thanks for letting me intrude on your special day."

Roman says nothing. He just stares at the now open box and I peer in. There's a watch in there, a silver band and the face of its green. It's pretty, not very Roman. But maybe he will wear it somewhere fancy. Oh, like graduation?

"Is that a real Rolex?" Walker asks casually. *It's a Rolex?*

"Why would I give someone a fake Rolex, Walker?" Alessandro seems a little offended at Walkers' remarks of it being real. Walker takes a step back and shrugs.

I can see people who don't have a lot of money giving fake ones. It's an honest question. My stepfather has one. Its real, it's gold. Don't like it much, but this one is much nicer. Elegant.

Everyone surrounds us now. Interested in the newcomer and the watch Roman's now holding. Now my gift seems crap in comparison. Not that I've given it to him yet. Mine's personal though and I know Roman will appreciate it. I put a lot of thought into it.

Asher comes up beside me and looks. He leans in close, "that's at least a thirty grand watch. Maybe more."

My mouth drops open. I can see why Walker questioned it. That's an insane gift to give someone. Roman's speechless. Hell, I almost forget words. I quickly clear my throat.

"Thank you, Alessandro. Roman's not a man of many words, and I think you've just shocked him speechless." Alessandro just grins and nods. Dang… that's a scary hot grin.

"It's the least I could do after everything. Now the reason that I'm here." I lean in a little closer and Alessandro eyes Emerson and Cadence. Then his eyes scan to Grady.

"Ah, let's go talk in private." I lead Alessandro over to the ball pit. The suit follows him. And Hunter, Roman, Asher, Walker, and Jace follow me. I guess we were all there that day, so it makes sense we all hear what he has to say.

"I spoke to my father; he was… not impressed." I suck in a breath. "That our family name had been used in such a manner. The problem has been dealt with. But you mentioned the cops sniffing around with our name in their mouth. My father wasn't happy to hear this and had it looked into."

I swallow down the lump in my throat. Is he here because he's angry that the cops are looking into the connection between us and his family? That's not our fault.

"My father has… *friends*. It's just a cop and his daughter looking into the connection between us. You might know her. She attends Ridgecrest high."

"Britney Montlake," Roman hisses under his breath.

Alessandro nods. "So, you know the girl. Her story is that she witnessed the murder of Damon Valentine, but named Roman as the killer. Not you Mila."

Alessandro tilts his head, gives me a once over, and raises his brows. "Honestly, from looking at you, I wouldn't think you could kill a person, even in self-defence. But you have a bit of a death wish about you, trying to break into my family's estate and all. But when you look at Roman…"

He didn't finish. I knew what he was implying. Roman looks big and strong enough to take down a man like this, father. Not me. What was there to say? Alessandro's right. But how would Britney know it was Roman? The three of us look to the only other person who knows what really happened that night.

Jace's eyes widen and he shakes his head. "No, don't look at me like that. We trust each other. I would never break your trust again, Mila. I swear to God I haven't said a thing to the cops or Britney."

Hunter speaks up, "Sorry man. Just so much going on and I thought it was you for a split second and I should've known you wouldn't betray us. But you came to us after Britney and the cops questioned you. We told you then. You had no idea beforehand."

"Plus, you're not that good of an actor." I add and smile. I feel bad for even thinking it could be Jace.

Jace lets out a deep breath and chuckles nervously. "That's why I don't do drama. All kinds."

It's then I realize Walker and Asher have been listening to everything. Their expressions reading, they know what we're talking about. Asher reaches out to me and I shake my head. I don't know what he wants to say, but I don't need it right now. I need to focus on how Britney knew this. Or did she guess?

"Alright, well, I'll be on my way now. Enjoy shooting each."

I think all our mouths drop open at that statement from Alessandro. He just chuckles and even that makes my stomach warn me he's a dangerous guy from a mob family. One that can kill and bury you and no one would ever find you again type of dangerous. And I have no intentions on being where Johnny and Carlos are right now.

Roman finally speaks up as Alessandro saunter towards the door of the building.

"We only have nine players, the tenth couldn't make it. If you want to stay around and play for a bit. You're welcome to join us."

My mouth drops open. I can't believe Roman just invited a mobster to play laser tag with us all. I'm more surprised that he said so many words to someone that's not me or the guys. Maybe it's the expensive watch, or maybe this is the new Roman. No longer having a shadow over him at every step. This is Roman free, living his life to the fullest.

Alessandro grins.

"Whose team am I on?"

Well, I hope he's on mine. I bet he knows his way around a gun.

Even if it is just a laser one.

NINETEEN
MILA

We draw names from a hat to pick the teams. Roman, by default, gets me first pick. Walker's the leader for the other team and pulls Cadence from the hat.

She smiles over at me shyly. Emerson see's this and if looks could kill. I think he might be a little jealous that she's on Walker's team.

"Quick, Roman. Pull the next name." Emerson shifts the weight on his feet. I cross my fingers, hoping that they can be on the same team together. Matchmaker me wanting this for Cadence. Even if it's so she can kiss him.

Roman grunts at Em's impatience and pulls out, "Emerson."

Em's face falls slightly, but then he claps Roman on the shoulder as he stands beside me. He gives me a small side hug. Alessandro's eyes are on me and Em. I don't like the way he watches me. Not every guy around me wants to date me.

Alessandro's lips tilt on one side. The way he looks at me under his lashes has me feeling a little flushed. I look away just as Walker pulls out another name.

"Grady."

Roman draws, "Alessandro."

I look over to him again and he smirks. *Oh, god.* Walker draws again.

"Hunter." I'm a little crestfallen he's not on our team. But he winks over at me as he high fives Walker. Oh, actually this is gonna be fun with us on different teams.

I watch as the two left—Jace and Asher— stare at the hat. They eye each other. Fuck, I don't want them to fight on who Roman draws out next. It's at random. It's not like he's doing it on purpose. But it's awkward that they are the two left. Jace smiles over at me, and I hold my breath. Asher tilts his head at me and gives a small smile.

Ugh, be still my heart. Seeing them both there is hard. I have feelings for them both and now I feel like this is going to leave one out if we don't pick him. Even though it's just a game.

Emerson notices the stand-off. Even Walker's watching Roman as he puts his hand in the hat to draw the next name, but he's taking a painfully long time to do so. Em takes my hand and pulls me in close and whispers.

"This is a little tense, and I don't even know why." I snort, holding my hand to my mouth as I try to hold in the laughter. He doesn't know about Asher. About my butterflies for them all.

"So, who is this guy and the suit?" he nods over at Alessandro, then to the guy in the suit standing nearby, who's talking into an earpiece. He's a bodyguard for a mobster son… there has to be a reason he has three of them. And I don't wanna know.

"Someone you would want to forget after tonight." I whisper back. The puzzled expression he gives, me makes me laugh a little. I purse my lips as I press my finger to his forehead and he relaxes.

"He's the son of a powerful mafia boss."

He looks to Alessandro, then to me, and back to him. I raise my brows when he burst out laughing. Why's he laughing?

"Nice play, Mila." He turns to Alessandro.

"Hey, I'm Emerson. I'm over at Ridgecrest." Holding his hand out for Alessandro. Who takes it and shakes it.

"Alessandro, I'm over at Royale Academy."

Em looks to me as if to say, you think you're funny. No, I'm just sick of lying.

"Mila just said your dad's a mafia boss." Then chuckled. "She likes to mess with me a lot. But I'm not falling for that." Em looks down at me. "And I'm the king of England."

"Oh, but he is." Alessandro smirks.

Emerson just laughs and clasps his hand on Alessandro's shoulder.

"Oh, you're a funny too. We are gonna get along just fine." Alessandro raises his brow at me, and I shrug. What can I say? Emerson is… well, he's Emerson. He's never claimed to be smart.

"Jace." Roman calls out and I turn, almost forgetting

what had been happening. Roman holds up the piece of paper with Jace's name on it and he whoops loudly before joining us.

Asher looks deflated, but when he sees me, he smiles. But it's not an innocent smile. It's a worrying one… what does he have planned?

W e all get suited up, and the owner—Jake —gives us our laser guns and the rules. Showing us how to aim and shoot the chest pieces and how it all works. How the points are tallied for the game Walker chose. It's pretty simple. First team to fifty kills is the winner. So we just have to not be killed and kill the other team to win… yeah, that seems easy. Once we are shot, we go back to the start and Jake will be there to count us down until we can get back into the game.

I like these rules, because I have a feeling I'm going to be the first to die and then I would be stuck on the sidelines for the rest of the game. Maybe Walker thought the same. The boys can play the other version later and all kill each other while Cadence and I eat all the candy.

I'm so nervous I think I need to pee. I've never done this before, but I'm so excited. I just don't want to be the first one shot.

We enter the doorway into the laser tag area. The blue lights make everything darker and there's glow in the dark paint on the walls and beyond on any obstacles.

My heart's pounding as the countdown starts and I run. Hiding behind a fake boulder. Making sure my gun is ready to go, I look to see where the other team is. I'm on the green team and Walker's team is blue. Our equipment shows who's who.

"Go," yells Jake and everything moves so fast. The guys are grunting and yelling. But there's also some laughter coming from all around me. I keep looking out, trying to work out who's who as they run past me. This is a lot harder than I thought it would be.

That's until I see a player peek out and I take my chance. Their chest changes to red after I shoot at them. I did it. I get excited and jump up and down. This isn't so hard. I watch as Alessandro stands up with the red chest. My mouth drops open.

I just shot my teammate.

"Mila," is all he says as he laughs on his way to the meeting point to reset himself. I can't believe I shot him. I was too focused on shooting someone. I didn't even stop to see who it was.

Roman comes up beside me. I'm glad to see him. I don't want our team to lose. I want to win for him.

"I'm terrible at this, sorry. You would be better without me on your team. I shot Alessandro."

He squeezes my hand. "I don't care how good you are or if we win. All I care about is that I'm with you. Thank you… for everything."

I kiss him. When he pulls away, I look down at his now red chest. I look behind him and Hunter has a huge grin. He puts his hands up and chuckles.

"Cheap shot, sorry." Then he runs off laughing.

Roman tilts my chin up to him and I study his eyes.

"Was worth the kiss. Now you want to get someone who's not on our team?" I chuckle and nod. I would love to shoot someone not on my team. That's how this game is supposed to go.

"There's a room over there with a bit of a maze. I saw Walker go in there before. Want to get him?"

Oh, hell yeah. I wanna go get him. Get up from my spot and quickly kiss Roman before I run and dart to the other room. The obstacles here are like a maze, just as Roman said. It's also quieter in here. I can hear my heavy breathing and my footsteps as I make my way through the wooden obstacles. Where is he?

I squeal when Walker jumps out and shoots me. "Gotcha, Mila," he chuckles deeply before running off to find someone else to kill.

"Ugh, I'm seriously terrible at this game." I mumble to myself as I make my way to the meeting point to reset myself.

Cadence is there with Grady. They both smile as I approach them.

"This is so much fun. I've shot four green players already, Mila." She laughs, bouncing on her toes.

"This is the third time I've been here," Grady shakes his head.

"Well, now I don't feel so bad. This is only my first time here. But I have shot one person… my teammate."

Cadence stops bouncing and bursts out laughing. Grady chuckles, but I give him my best stink eye and point at him.

"Sorry, Mila. I shouldn't have laughed. It's just… we

have colors." Pointing to her chest where it's still red. "How did you not see your own teammate's chest before you shot him?"

I shake my head and laugh. "I was over eager?"

That lands a laugh, even from Jake. Their chests turn blue and they both run back into the game again as I wait for mine to turn green.

Jake shows me the security screens of the whole laser tag. I can see Cadence stalking after Roman. Asher and Hunter teaming up against Alessandro. Jake and points to a screen of the maze. No one appears on the screen there.

"He was hiding there." I look in closer to where I'd been shot by Walker. "No one's in there right now, but if you crouch low and hide behind there. You can ambush someone easily. Or you could just run in there, guns blazing. Either way, it's just in good fun."

I smile at Jake. He's not old. Maybe thirties? He has a scruffy beard, and deep blue eyes. He's nice and very helpful and hasn't mentioned anything about the three guys in suits.

"Thank you. I think I will take your advice."

He gives me a friendly smile. "Have fun and look for blue chests before you shoot."

I let out a deep breath and shake my head, but I can't wipe the grin from my face. Last week, we were too busy looking over our shoulder and wondering when Johnny and Carlos would strike next.

But today, we're all relaxed, smiling and laughing. Having fun. Just like we used to as kids.

I hold my laser gun in my hand, salute Jake as I run

back into the game. I go into full kamikaze mode. As soon as I see a blue chest, I shoot and run towards them. When it turns red, I whoop loudly. Hunter stands there dumbfounded. I grin wildly at him and run to find another blue team member. Didn't realize how big this place was until you're lost in the laser tag maze again. I hide where Jake told me, waiting for a blue player to come past me.

When I see one, I jump up to surprise them. One shot is all it takes, and Grady's chest glows red.

"Far out. I'm officially the most shot at player in this game." I laugh. At least I've only been out once. I finally shot two blue players and I feel like I'm on top of the world.

I hide back down again and wait, feels like forever, but it's probably been only a few minutes. I hear someone approaching, but they're coming from a different direction, and I can't pinpoint exactly where they're gonna come out from. This maze is easy to get lost in.

As soon as the footsteps are close enough, I jump out. Only I don't expect to see their laser gun pointed right at my chest. Just as mine points to his.

I look up and see Asher. He grins. It's one of those sexy ones and I feel hot all of a sudden. My breathing picks up a little and I look to his laser.

"I got you, Mila."

He hasn't shot me yet. I don't know why. But I'm going to use that to my advantage. If I'm affected this easily by him. He's gotta be the same way with me.

"No, you wouldn't shoot, poor little old me." I bat my lashes at him and he chuckles.

"Mmm… looks like we have a standoff." Asher grins.

"Is that so?" I cock my hip and look up at him. In the blue lights he looks good… so handsome. He always looks good, especially when he doesn't have a shirt on.

I lick my lips as he moves closer. He taps his gun gently to my chest and I take a step back, as if that would stop him from being able to shoot me.

"You like me too much to shoot me," I flirt. Looking up at him through my lashes.

"Ah, I think you have me confused with Hunter. I have no qualms about shooting you. No matter how much I like you, I also enjoy winning."

He moves a step forward, and I take one back. *Fuck*. As soon as I shoot him, he's gonna shoot me. I just know it.

"But you haven't shot me yet. So there must be a reason for that."

I keep backing up until my back hits a wall. My heart races. The way he's looking down at me in the dark room is making my butterflies dance low in my belly… *very low*.

We stand there, watching each other. Our breathing is the only sound between us and the race of my heart pounding in my chest. The laser guns are still pointed at each other's chests. Only now we're so close they almost touching. The blue of his and the green of mine glow between us.

"Asher," I warn. This is not the time or place for this. Hell, I still need to speak to him about what dad said this morning. About asking his mom to marry him. because that will complicate things between us.

"Mila," he purrs. *Fuck.* I'm so fucked right now.

"Shoot me," he takes my hand that's holding the laser gun and presses it firmly to his chest. "Or can't you either?"

He bites his lower lip as he bends down to my ear and whispers "You like me too much to shoot me."

I gasp at his words. And I wanna wipe that smirk right off his face. He pulls away from me slightly. His chest goes from blue to red as I pull the trigger. I don't speak, just frozen in this place between him and what's out there. I watch his eyes widen as his mouth drops open, that I actually did it. His eyes find mine and darken. And my body react to it. my body leans towards him, my chest now pressing against his.

"Mila," he groans. My mouth grows dry and I swallow and try to right myself and my emotions. Is it hot in here? It's hot right?

Asher doesn't move, he just stands there and stares down at me. The butterflies in my stomach growing stronger by the minute, and I want them to stay away. Just for tonight. This is Roman's special party. I can't be doing this right now but my body's reacting to him, even if my mind tells me not to.

"We can't. Not here. *Not now.* We need to talk… later" I beg him and I know those words hurt him. I can see it in is eyes. His jaw ticks as he glances behind him.

When he turns back the dark expression is back and the corner of his lip tilts up.

Asher shoots my chest, and it turns red.

"What the hell, Asher. You can't just shoot me"

He doesn't say a word. He's upset with me. For stopping this… again and again. I'm upset that we keep ending up like this. Dancing around each other, flirting and getting all hot then me shutting it down.

I feel guilty for wanting him… I shouldn't and I can't stop. Only now our faces are so close our breath mingles. My breathing speeds up and I swallow the lump in my throat. I don't know what to say. He's affecting me in a way that my mind screams to kiss him, but my heart says no wait, not here. Not tonight.

His free hand grips the back of my neck, and he's warm lips crash into mine as I let out a gasp. My hand grabs his chest, to push him away. But I don't. I pull his body flush to mine chasing the ecstasy that's his kiss.

I moan as his tongue meets mine. All sense of space and time disappear. I drop my laser gun and put my arm around his neck. Pulling him closer to me, chasing the kiss, the need, this thing that has been building up between us for so long. And now it's tipped over. He devours me, leaving me breathless.

I know this is wrong. In the back of my mind. But no one can see us here. I will talk with Hunter and Roman about Asher. That I need him, I can't keep denying this between us. I can't give him up. *I won't*. It's been building for so long, and now it's tipped over. I can't stop kissing him.

Roman gave me a half blessing when he was outside Alessandro's house.

But Hunter, he hasn't given me his blessing. I can't do this to him, not until he says so. I shove Asher away. And touch my swollen lips as I breath deeply.

"I'm not sorry, I know you're not either. They'll understand. They feel it too, what I feel for you. I love you." Asher's big dark eyes are full of emotion. He's opening up to me and I need to do the same.

My heart's exploding with the words. *I love you.* When I open my mouth, there are no words. I take Asher's hand in mine. Hunter and Roman are behind him now watching me. Staring at us. I can't even see their expressions in the dark. But from the way Roman's standing… he's not happy. My stomach drops.

The guilt I feel eats up all the happiness I had from that kiss.

Those words.

Roman storms over and grabs the back of Asher's top. He pulls him away from me and I reach out to stop him from falling on the floor. But Hunter's there to catch him. Roman hauls me over his shoulder and stomps away. I turn just in time to watch Hunter slam his fist into Asher's face.

"Don't," I yell out to Hunter. But Asher just smiles and nods that it's okay. It's not okay. This shouldn't be happening. This is all my fault. I shouldn't have kissed him. I knew this would end badly, but I didn't walk away.

Fucking butterflies.

Everyone looks at us and stops what they are doing.

They follow us outside of the laser tag area and into the bright lights of the arcade. I blink a few times to get used to the light.

Roman gently places me on my feet. His hand large and warm cups my face. I can't look him in the eye. I've ruined his party. I kissed Asher.

"Mila," he pulls my face to look up at him. He gives me a smile that doesn't reach his eyes. He's not mad, but he's not happy either. I shake my head.

"I'm sorry, Roman. I didn't mean for it to happen like that. It's never happened before." He just grunts. A tear slips from my eye, and he wipes it away with the pad of his thumb. That only made way for more tears.

"Don't cry, Mila." He whispers. "I'm not upset with you. I've known this will happen for a long time. Just seeing it…" He lets out a deep breath. "It was hard. But you want him, yes? He means a lot to you?"

I nod. "Yes, he does."

"Then that's all I need to hear." He kisses my forehead and pulls me to his chest, hugging me tightly. "Don't cry beautiful, I understand. I love you, and if you want him, then he'll be yours."

My mouth drops open, and I sniffle a little.

"But right now, you're mine. He's gonna need to learn to share."

I think Roman's gonna need to learn to share too. But that's for another day.

I hear yelling as Hunter and Asher exit the laser tag. I turn to see blood running down Asher's face. He's bleeding.

He meets my eyes and smiles. But another set of

tears come. I don't want them to fight over me. This isn't what I had planned. I hate this. I hate I love them all. My eyes widen at that thought. I have never admitted that before, even in my head I've never thought about it. But I do. I love Asher, Roman, Hunter and Jace.

"It was worth it, Mila." Asher calls over to me. "I would do it again in a heartbeat."

"Shut up, if you know what's good for you." Walker warns him.

Everyone's quiet and I realize then, that I've ruined the whole party vibe.

"Well, this has been entertaining." Alessandro smirks at me. "I think your fourth has become your third."

Jace curses and looks between Asher and me.

Fuck.

I look at Hunter and he shakes his head with a small smile.

"We need to talk about this. It's all good, babe."

Asher smiles reassuringly as he presses some tissues around his nose. He holds his hand over his heart and nods to me.

My phone rings and I look down to see my dad's name on the caller id. *Fuck…* how could I forget? He's gonna be my stepbrother.

Why do I suddenly feel like I just made everything more complicated than it needed to be? Why does he have to be my stepbrother?

How am I gonna tell my dad? How do I tell Kate? Why do I get myself into these messes?

But I look over at Asher, and I realize he's worth the mess. At least I hope so.

"I'm going to be grounded forever." I mutter.

Asher chuckles.

"Me too, but at least we'll be grounded together."

TWENTY
JACE

"'m so glad you boys could make it today." Mom hugs Hunter and walks around the table to Roman. He's never hugged mom before, but he stands and wraps his arms around my mother. She's dwarfed by his size.

"Oh, Roman. I have cake for you." She sniffles and I know she's getting emotional. I can't do this right now. We have plans and they involve a knife and Asher. I don't want to do cake. It won't be the same without Mila here. And well… Asher.

"Okay, mom. We gotta go do thanksgiving at Hunter's now. So, we will see you tomorrow."

She's not happy that I'm bailing out on thanksgiving so early, but I explained to her that Hunter's mom wasn't well so we would do lunch with mom, dad, and Grady. Plus, the guys. Then go to Hunter's later. I haven't seen his mom in weeks… but then I've been a little preoccupied trying to get Mila to kiss me. So, I hope she's not there to witness that.

But tonight's gonna be the night Mila kisses me. I'm gonna make her want to kiss me. That's what happened with Asher. She said so herself. That it built and built until it spilled over into a kiss at the laser tag. "Epic kiss." Were her exact words and I want to top that.

Who wants epic when you can have legendary.

Well, okay, I'm gonna work on my kiss after Roman's had his special birthday gift from Mila. He's made it clear we are not to go near her room. For at least half the night. I don't know how Hunter's not jealous because I sure am. But I gotta hold that in. If I want her, I have to share her. Just going to take some time to get used to all of it.

"Take leftovers, and the cake." Mom packs everything up into Tupperware containers while we wait for her in the kitchen. I message Asher letting him know to meet us at Hunter's place in ten.

"You say hi to your parents from us, Hunter. Haven't seen them in so long. Your father's always working so hard."

Yeah… you could say that. Working so hard, he's never around. But Hunter just smiles and tells dad he will pass on the message. I know he won't. Not because he doesn't want to. But because he won't see his dad for so long, he will have forgotten it by then. I really don't like his dad.

Grady gives the guys a small hug and leaves the room. Probably to go call his boyfriend. Well… he hasn't told me if it's official, but he's been seeing Makai. At least openly around our house. Not so openly at school, but he doesn't have to. Until yesterday, Roman didn't kiss Mila in public. But now everyone knows.

So, I can understand Grady wanting privacy. Because that shit was crazy.

W e all jump into Hunter's car. I can't wipe the smile from my face. This is going to hurt like hell. But Asher wants to do it. That's the only way that Roman and Hunter will give their blessing for him to date Mila.

"So, you've got the knife?" I ask Roman, who's sitting in the back seat with his bag. He pats it.

"Yeah, the same one. If he's going to be one of us, this is the only way." I nod and agree.

Asher was told he needs to be a blood brother. It's the only way. Or he'll always be the outsider.

I'm glad that with age, the sight of blood doesn't affect me anymore, but there's no way that I could make that cut on Asher without vomiting. Roman offered to do it soon as it was mentioned. Said it had to be him. After all, he was the one who came up with the original idea.

When we pull into Hunter's property. Asher's standing there waiting for us. He's wearing all black. That's a smart choice. Roman chuckles deeply. It's a little evil. But I like it. I feel the same way.

We pile out of the car and I wave over to Asher to follow me. It's dark now and the full moon's out. But we use the flashlights on our phones to guide us into the yard where it all began four years ago.

"Do you think we should have invited Mila?" I whisper to Hunter. I only just realized now that it's not exactly the same without her there.

Hunter pauses for a second then looks back to Asher. He shakes his head.

"No, this has to be done without her. She wants him. He gives her butterflies. This is where we make him work for her. If he really wants in, he'll do this."

Asher overhears us and replies.

"I want this to work. I want to be with Mila, and I understand this is the way it has to be for you guys."

Roman calls for us to hurry up. I would say he's a little impatient but it's his birthday and he wants to see Mila. We track our way through the backyard and into the spot where it all began. Roman drops his backpack onto the dirt and pulls out the knife.

Asher takes a step back, then shakes his head, holding his hands up.

"Okay, I didn't know there was a knife involved." He turns pale in the moonlight. Roman chuckles, think this is more for him than the rest of us. Hell, I'm thinking Mila has no idea what's going on. This is the Roman show. I'm just along for the ride.

"How did you think we got the blood brother scars? Mila has one on her palm too. They're identical. We made a pact to be together forever. If you want this. If you truly want to be with Mila. You will be part of this and wear the scar on your palm." Roman explains to him.

"Don't worry, football season's over. You have me to contend with next season. So, if you don't heal up, I have no problems taking your spot on the team." Hunter jokes with him.

Asher mumbles. "Fuck, I didn't think about that."

Hunter laughs. "Yeah, I'm not a quarterback like Jace. I'm a wide receiver dude and you're in my spot." I look to Asher and then back to Hunter. This isn't what we came here to do. I'm sure they will work something out at Lakeview. Maybe Asher can play a different position?

"Alright, let's get this over with because Roman has a date tonight with a very special lady and it's cold out here." I didn't want to wait around here any longer. And I sure as hell didn't want to hear them fighting over who was going to be the wide receiver for the King's next season.

I didn't even want to think about Hunter not being a Rebel anymore. Hell, this time next week he won't even be attending Ridgecrest high anymore.

I fucking hate his dad for doing this. Splitting us up like this. Doesn't matter what school you go to. Education is education.

Roman flicks the knife out, the silver of it gleans in the moonlight. I hear Asher take a small intake of breath. I realize now that we made another mistake about this. We all did it together. As in we pressed our palms together to make the blood pact.

But that's another thing Roman doesn't care about. He said this was the only way, and I believe him. But now everything is piecing together, and I think this might have a little bit more to do with the kiss last night.

I'd been a little upset that Mila had kissed Asher before she kissed me. So, I thought this was a good idea when Roman suggested it. I remember that knife and that hurt like a bitch.

"Do you want this? do you really want this?" Roman asks Asher.

"Yes, I've told you I do. She's it for me. I don't care how young we are. I just know it in my bones. I love her."

Roman nods, then punches Asher in the stomach and he keels over and groans. Hunter gives me a confused look, but Roman nods for us to come over. What the hell is going on?

"Hunter, it's your turn," and Asher stands up. Getting ready for another blow.

Okay, this is new as well. No one told me that this is how it was going down. I wish they would talk to me more, so we'd all be on the same page coming here, not this. Hunter hits him in the stomach, only this time Asher drops to his knees and hisses out in pain.

Hunter looks to me, and he doesn't even have to say a word. I know what to do. I'm going to enjoy it, just a little. Asher can be a cocky asshole, but he seems to have soften around Mila. He gets to his feet, but this time. He tries to stand tall, but the pain he's in won't let him. I hit him in the same spot, only I give him a soft blow. He groans but keeps standing.

I eye Hunter, but he just shrugs. Okay, I guess that wasn't just new to me and Roman took some creative flare. He needs to tone it down. Mila's gonna rip him a new one if she finds out.

"Hold your hand out," Asher gives his right hand over to Roman. Then quickly changes his mind to his left.

"Good idea." I tell him. Or he won't be jerking off with that hand for weeks.

Roman takes his hand in his and looks Asher in the eye.

"Do you promise to take care of Mila? Protect each other, our secrets, and our lives. Blood friends for life." The words are new and old. Mixed with the words of our past and ones of our future.

"I promise." Asher says, and I can hear in his voice his wants this. He really does love Mila..

"Blood Brothers." Hunter cheers and I follow.

"Blood Brothers for life," Roman calls out as he draws the blade across Asher's palm.

Asher lets out a hiss and grunt, as he stumbles forward looking down at his hand. The blood pools there. He clenches it, trying his best to stop it. But it just runs down his wrist. Shit, we should have brought a towel to stop the bleeding.

"Congratulations, blood brother." I'm the first to say, as I grab his shoulder and squeeze it.

"Blood brother for life." Hunter hugs him from the side. Avoiding the blood. I look down and wonder what went through his mind to wear pure white shoes out here. Hunter's very anal about his shoes and there's dirt back here… and now blood..

Roman grunts as he digs a hole and buries the knife in the dirt.

"Blood brothers." He pats Asher on the back.

Look back to where the knife's now buried. I point to it. I hadn't seen it since we all did this with Mila.

"Was that buried there before? For the past four years and you dug it up?" Hunter nods.

"Yeah, he dug it up earlier. Look at all the holes. He couldn't remember exactly where he buried it. Was like finding a treasure."

Huh. I didn't realize he had buried it back then. But then at the same time. I hadn't seen it in four years. He cleaned it up before he cut Asher, right? I looked to Asher and decide to hold that question until I'm alone with Roman.

"So, is that how it went back when Mila was with you and you all did it together?" Asher asks. He holds his hand now. Probably to stop the bleeding but its not much help.

"More or less," I reply.

"Less Jace fainting and more punching this time." Hunter chuckles, and Asher's mouth drops open.

"Wait up. Are you telling me you all hit me, and it's not a part of it?"

"Not originally no, that was a last-minute change." Roman says. I can see him hiding a grin. Asher makes a sound and I feel bad… just a little for the guy. He did kiss Mila first.

"Very last minute. I didn't even realize it was gonna happen." I reply.

Asher doesn't look impressed with that, but what can he say? It's already happened and now he's one of us.

"That won't happen again, you're one of us now." Roman states.

But I'm not sure that sounds convincing to Asher. He looks at us all and shakes his head.

"Okay, so this means I can be with Mila now and you're all good with it?"

Hunter nods and Roman grunts. I raise my hand.

"No, I'm not good with it because I'm not with her. I was supposed to be next, but you jumped your turn. We were supposed to go me, then you." I kick the dirt on the ground and fill one hole that Roman dug earlier.

"I'm not sorry," Asher smirks, and I shrug.

"What can I say? She picked you and not me. But tonight, I'm going to fix that. She's going to kiss me. I just know it."

"Yeah, after she sucks Roman's cock." Hunter chuckles. Fuck no. Before that. I don't want to taste that in my mouth. Okay, sharing's going to be more than interesting. Lots of teeth brushing… yet is that enough to not taste my friend's cum in her mouth? How do Hunter and Roman do this?

"We also have to have a rule chat about group times together with her, because now there are eight arms and four dicks. Only one Mila."

I stop kicking the dirt and look over to Hunter. What the…

"Let me get this straight. Are you talking about group sex?" I'm so lost right now.

"Yes, that's exactly what I'm talking about because now there's more of us, chances are we might accidentally touch each other."

Holy shit. Hunter and Roman have been sharing her in and out of the bedroom. That didn't even cross my mind.

"But we'll talk about that later. It's Roman's birthday and Mila has a present to give him." Hunter says as he walks back towards the car.

Asher holds his hand and follows. I fall back beside him. He drove here, and I don't think he's gonna make it back with that cut.

"Hey, I'll drive you back. Then when we get back to your place, I'll help you with the first aid kit." I don't want his hand getting all infected or Mila seeing it.

"Thanks for not hitting so hard." He replies and I chuckle.

"I knew you were gonna get cut, so I took it easy on you."

I hope Mila doesn't see Asher's hand and freak out.

Chances are… *she will.*

TWENTY-ONE
MILA

I jump, I spin, I wave my arm in the air. Madison does the same beside me.

"Oh my God, I think we got," she turns her phone to playback the TikTok dance we just made together.

"If it's not, I give up." I say as I slide into the armchair. Dancing takes a lot out of you.

"You're the good one. I'm crap. That's why I have to keep doing it. But don't give up. This is fun." She bounces around, humming the song we'd just been dancing to.

I'm exhausted. We've been at this for most today. As much as I love Madison, this is just too much, and I need a break. She seems to be full of energy. Maybe it's that I can't stop thinking of Asher's kiss last night. And my mind's in another place. Not TikTok dancing.

I hear the front door of the house open and the laughter of the guys spills into the hallway. Echoing off the walls in the living room.

"We're in here," I call to them.

Roman told me they were taking Asher to have a bonding afternoon with him. But I wasn't too sure how long of a day they would need, but just grateful that Hunter and Roman are okay with this. With me and Asher. I take a sip of water from the water bottle, then wait for them to appear.

When they do, it's not the vision I thought I would be. Asher's holding his bleeding hand and gives a half wave as he moves away from the living room. Jace follows him out. And I stand there dumbfounded.

"Blood Brothers?" I narrow my eyes at Roman and then back to Hunter.

"Seriously guys, that took ages to heal. Why would you do that to him?"

"It was a test, and he passed it. Will have that scar for life and, at least, have a special memory behind it like ours." Hunter smiles and I grumble in my chest.

"Don't worry, I'm gonna go take care of him." Jace yells out from where very he is. I don't know if that's better or not.

I make my way over to Roman and slap him on the chest.

"Happy birthday, but you shouldn't have done that." He just gives a half shrug, as if that was completely normal. It's not normal to go cutting people's hands in a blood pact. But when's anything normal with these guys? *With us.*

But it's his birthday, so I forget all that's happened tonight and jump into his arms. He catches me and I see his smile as he grips my ass.

"Take me to my room. I can show you my birthday present for you."

He slaps my ass, and I jump in his arms and giggle. There's two parts to my present. One is the actual present, the other is also for me.

Madison waves as she watches Roman practically jog to my bedroom.

As soon as we're in my room, he slams the door and his lips crush to mine. I break the kiss as I drop from his arms. I back up a little so I can take him in. His present can come second. I can't stand another minute of not touching him.

I pull my sweater off and look at his reaction. I'm wearing a red lace bra, I bought specially for this occasion. He growls in the back of his throat when I drop the sweats. I grin. I turn around slowly so he can see all of it.

"Happy birthday, handsome."

I stalk over to him and tug on the ends of his ash blonde hair until our lips press together. I gasp as his tongue meets mine. His arms around me, pulling me flush to his body and I can feel all the hard plains of his abs.

His hands go to my ass, and he lifts me up against him. My core aches as wetness pools between my thighs.

I want to drown in Roman.

My hands go to his face, only now I don't hesitate. I touch him. He pulls me closer, deepening our kiss. And

I rub shamelessly against the fly on his jeans. Moaning from the pleasure it gives me as he kisses all the sounds from my mouth.

He breaks the kiss, and I lick my lips, missing the taste of him already. My breathing's shallow. Slowly, I run my hand from his face to his chest. His heart's racing, but so is mine.

"Tell me this isn't a dream." He whispers to me. My heart skips a beat.

"If this is a dream, I don't wanna wake up." I reply honestly.

He leans in and nips at my ear, tracing kisses down the column of my throat. His fingers trace down my collarbone to my aching breasts where he cups one, brushing his thumb over my hard nipple. I can feel that all the way to my core.

"Oh, God. Mila." He groans my name. Pushing my chest into his palm. I want more. I need everything he can give me.

He pushes down the straps of my bra and his tongue dips to my collarbone. I softly moan as he grinds his erection against my stomach. Walking me towards the bed he placing me gently on the soft sheets.

He takes a step back and I reach for him, I need him so bad. But he shakes his head.

"Let me just look at you for a moment. You're so beautiful, Mila." My butterflies dance at the words.

"I love you, Mila Hart. I want to make love with you tonight." The breath catches in my throat. I wasn't expecting those words. But I want that, I want to feel him.

He pulls a condom from his jeans pocket, and I shake my head.

"I'm protected. We don't need that if you don't want to." He groans as he throws it onto my nightstand.

"You're killing me, Mila. I'm barely keeping control now." He presses the heel of his palm into the large bulge in his jeans.

I don't move from where I am. Watching as he slowly strips out of his clothes, his eyes never breaking from mine. Until he's standing there naked like a Greek God, his hard cock in his hand, slowly stroking the monster that it is.

He looks to it, then to me.

"I don't want to hurt you." He almost whispers in the quiet room. I shake my head.

"You won't hurt me, it'll feel good." He doesn't seem as convinced as me. He slowly approaches me and grabs my knee, pushing it up to my chest.

He rubs his fingers over my lace song, feeling the wetness pooling there between my thighs. I moan his name as he strums over my clit.

I hope he doesn't wanna tease me for too long, because I can't wait to feel him inside me.

"Come to me, Roman." I reach to him, he lets me pull him onto the bed. I scoot up, so we're both now in the middle. He lays his weight against me, his cock nestling between my thighs, and presses up on his elbows a little to help me breathe.

"God, you're so tiny, Mila. I don't want to break you." As if that's even possible.

"Take off my underwear."

He sits up and fumbles nervously with my thong, so I help him with my bra. I throw it across the room. It hits the wall it slides down into a pile that's been forming there the past week. I never claimed to be clean.

I want to touch his cock. I want to make him feel good. But I suspect he's just as worked up as me. So, I run my fingers down his chest and he watches me but doesn't push me away.

"Only you." He says as he watches me toy with his nipple.

"Only me?"

"Can touch me like that. When it's you, all the bad thoughts go away. With you Mila, everything's perfect. You're everything I've ever wanted. And I know I'm bad with words…" he trails off, but I tilt his chin to get him to look at me again.

"You're not bad. I'm loving every word you say right now. You're opening up more than ever and I love that you trust me to let me in."

He studies my face, his fingers brushing over my eyelids, my cheeks and nose. I lick his finger when he gets close to my mouth, and he smiles.

"I love you, Mila. I trust you with my life. I would lay mine down for yours. You always saw more in me, even when I couldn't see it myself. I wasn't some poor kid from a bad family with a chip on his shoulder. You saw me. The real me inside." He taps his chest over his heart. "From that day, I knew I would make you mine. And you're mine Mila. *Always*."

I pull him down and his hard cock nestles now on

my bare flesh. As I kiss him, I rock my hips against his velvety length. A need pulsates between my legs.

"I love you, Roman Valentine."

He moans as I take his mouth again and reach between us. Taking his cock in my hand, he breaks from the kiss and looks down between us. I open my legs wider to accommodate his frame as I line him up.

I don't move. I let him decide if this is what he wants.

But it doesn't take long. His hips flex…

TWENTY-TWO
ROMAN

My beautiful Mila, lays spread out like an angel beneath me. I still feel like I'm dreaming, and even if I am. This will always be one of my favourite memories. My first-time making love to my girl. *My Mila.*

She's breathtaking, absolutely stunning and I don't know how I became so lucky to have ever have someone like her in my arms. Loving me, as I love her,

My breathing speeds up as I look to where she holds my hard cock at her entrance. I watch her chest rise and fall. She's just as worked up as me.

But she's beautiful. She really is my Angel.

I'm nervous, but I don't have to tell her, she already knows. But my hips flex. My body knows what to do. I feel her wet heat as my cock nestles within her core. I still for a moment as she let out a small gasp, worried that I've hurt her.

"Don't stop, it feels amazing."

"I could say the same." I rumble deep in my chest. I

look to where we are connected, and slowly sink deep within her. It feels like a tight warm vice around my hard cock, I've never felt anything like this before. I'm glad that I waited for Mila. This is better than I ever knew. I bend down and kiss her and she returns my kisses. Moaning, she arches her back pressing her breasts into my chest.

"Make love to me," she whispers. I pull out and slowly stroke back into her again she groans in pleasure, and I do the same.

I move so I can look down, watching with each thrust. My cock disappearing. In and out. The pleasure growing. But I know it's not enough, not enough for her. Slow is not what we need. We need harder, faster.

I pick up the pace a little, finding different movements bring out different sounds from her. I pull myself back from her till I'm sitting on my knees I look down to her pussy. I run the pad of my thumb over her clit. She clenches tight around me and I feel like she's trying to strangle my cock. I groan as the orgasm grows closer. My spine tingles with the warning I'm close. Very close to coming.

"Oh god, Roman. Fuck me." She moans and I don't think about it. I do what she asks of me. I will do anything for her.

My hips flex and pump. Over and over, the sound of our breathing and the slapping of flesh-on-flesh echoes around the room as I chase after both our pleasure.

"I'm close." She calls out, and her fingers rubs her clit. I watch her, not pushing her hand away. As she chases the same high I'm on. But I watch to understand how to please her better. Because less than a minute later and I'm coming. I grunt and groan out my release. She curses as her pussy tightens around me and I lose all rhythm. *Holy shit*. My body bucks into hers, over and over as she drains my balls dry.

I collapse onto her and roll over enough so she can breathe. My limbs no longer work and my cock twitches happily still inside her.

I close my eyes and she peppers kisses all over my face. Pushing my hair back and playing with it as I slowly drift off to sleep hugging her to my chest.

When I wake, its cold where Mila had been. I look around the dark room and it's empty. I almost forget where I am for a moment. I reach over to find my phone and I feel a piece of paper crumple under my weight. I pull it up to read it, squinting in the dark.

When your finished dreaming of me. Come downstairs for a late night snack. Xx

smile down at her handwriting. I'm still in the dream. It's real.

I hear laughing and roll out of bed. I pick up my boxers from where I'd dropped them earlier. I want to be with her right. Sleep can come later, when she's with me.

I see a notebook, my name on the front. Is this my birthday present?

I open the notebook and see her sketches. She has so many. She's so talented. There's a page marked, and I flip to it and see my name. But on closer look I see it says Romeo. I roll my eyes. *Pinkie.*

But beside it my names spelt correctly. It's surrounded by daisies and a heart.

I feel her behind me as she wraps her arms around my waist and peers round to the sketch.

"I want you to give me that, tattoo me. For your birthday." I look down into her blue eyes and she beams back at me.

"That's if you want. Either way, that's going on my body. I just prefer you do it. That's why I didn't get it yet."

I kiss her. She wants my name on her body. I'm speechless as I kiss her. Trying to form words.

"I love you and I love it. I will do it. I don't have my own equipment. I'll have to do it down at the shop." The shop that I haven't been to for over a month. *At least.*

I haven't seen Ronnie since the funeral. He still needs to know if I will take over the shop while he is gone next year. I need to talk to everyone about that before I go deciding. These things don't just affect me now. They affect all of us.

"That's okay. I can wait till you're ready. Just know I love you, and I want to wear your name on my body. So all that sees me, will know I love you. That you're mine."

I growl and lift her up in my arms, desperately trying to hold my emotions at bay. But I can't. I kiss her fiercely.

"Thank you for my birthday present."

She rubs against me and purrs into my ear.

"I need you… again."

I'm not saying no to that. I spank her ass and take her to the bed. She moans my name as I kiss her.

"I never want to wake up from this." She says.

Me too.

TWENTY-THREE
MILA

t's been two weeks since Thanksgiving, and that night with Roman. Which I've repeated more times than I can count on my hands. It's like I woke the beast within him and I'm not complaining.

Hunter's now at Lakeview, he's giving Asher a run for his money. I'm glad they have each other there. Or from Walker's texts… maybe not. I guess they're very similar so they are butting heads a little.

Asher and I are stealing kisses. But that's all. I can't do anything else. Not yet. And not after dad and Kate announced their engagement. I don't want anything to stop them from being happy and married. I just need more time. Dad's still hung up on the fact I have two boyfriend's. I don't think he's going to bring out the welcome wagon for the one that lives across the hall from me.

Jace on the other hand… he's playing dirty and so am I.

It's movie night, just the five of us at Hunter's. Jace

wants to sit beside me, which would be no big deal only he's been slowly dragging his hand up my inner thigh. As if I wouldn't notice.

I get up to get more popcorn from the kitchen and he follows me. Ugh… well if he wants to play dirty… dirty's what he'll get.

He watches me as I stalk over, licking my lips and tasting the salt of the popcorn from them.

"Did you come to help?" I hand him the popcorn bowl and his eyes drop to my chest. I'm only wearing underwear under this tee. Which belongs to Roman, so it's big like a dress and that's exactly how I'm wearing it.

Jace stands a little taller as I move in. Only inches from him and he looks down at where I trace my finger down his tight tee and to the edge of his shorts. I watch his Adams apple bob, as I push my hand into his shorts and his breath comes out ragged as I press my palm against his hard length.

"Oh fuck," he whispers reaching for me, but I pull away as soon as he touches me. He lets go of my arm and I grip him through the thin fabric. He grips my shoulders again and moans. I work his length and his breathing picks up

"Please, god, Mila. Kiss me. I can't wait any longer. I need you."

I look up at him through my lashes and he's eyes widen. I stroke him one more time before yanking my hand free and skip towards the living room past Hunter. He must have come in here to get something, but instead witness Jace not getting what he wants.

Again. This has been happening since I kissed Asher…
well Asher kissed me and I kissed him back.

I know I'm being a bitch. But I think one more week
and it will be enough torture… *maybe.*

The deep groan from Jace has Hunter in a fit of
laugher.

"Shut up." Jace mutters but even I smile.

"You're only doing it to yourself by playing dirty.
You know the rules. You know what you did… and I
told you, paybacks a bitch."

I point to Hunter to come over to me, but he shakes
his head. I asked him where his mom is earlier, and
she's still at some retreat. Then I asked when his dad
was here, as feel like I have been living here for the past
two weeks and I haven't seen his dad once in that time.
He didn't answer me and I know there's more to it. But
he's avoiding me.

I'll let it slide for now. But later… he's gonna need to
answer me.

I enter the living room, and Asher looks up at me.
Roman had cuddles earlier and at the moment… that's
pretty much all Asher gets from me. Until we can work
out how to approach the parentals about the situation, I
don't want us to do more than kiss… cuddle and maybe
a little bit of touching.

I look down at the bandage still wrapped around
Asher's hand.

He told his mom it was an accident in the kitchen,
but it got infected. And more than that, when we ask
Roman about the knife and if he disinfected it. He just

looked at us and said, "it's a knife and I washed it." Like that's the answer to that.

But turns out he didn't know that after it was buried there for four years, it had rusted a little. He just washed it off in the pool. Yeah, the pool, then cut Asher's hand with it.

We had to explain how that's not the proper way to prepare a knife to cut something.

"How's your hand?"

"Needs kisses." I giggle and kiss him. It's been his line for the past week and it's cute. He's cute and mine.

His phone rings, and I realise that we're late home. We're picking out a Christmas tree today.

As a family.

love the smell of pine. It reminds me of Christmas. While I'd been living with mom; we didn't really celebrate Christmas the traditional way. She was more interested in socialite parties than a Christmas tree. If it wasn't for Malcolm, I wouldn't have had a Christmas at all in New York.

That's one thing he's good about at. Making sure that Malcolm junior and I had gifts. Even if they were bought by his secretary. He still at least thought about me to shop, not like my mother, who's never bought me a Christmas gift.

"Let's go pick out the perfect tree," Kate claps her hands after we all pile out the car.

I see a weird and ugly tree all by itself in the lot.

"Oh, my God, Kate, there it is." I point and run to it. Oh, the poor thing, it has a broken branch, and it's got a slight kink in the trunk.

Kate turns and gives me a puzzled look.

"Oh, no. Mila. We can afford the regular trees. We don't need the damaged one." Dad's phone rings and he looks at me before answering it. I pause a moment before I explain to Kate.

"It's not *damaged*, it just needs some TLC and it will be good for us. It needs a home for Christmas."

Kate looks to Asher, who shrugs. Then to Madison, who hasn't said much today. She's been really quiet and I want to ask her why, but when Kate and dad aren't around.

"Mila, it's an ugly tree." Madison screws her nose up at it. And I smile.

"I know. Isn't he perfect?" I sigh.

Dad comes over and smiles at me and my tree.

"It's the perfect tree, Mila. But we are choosing as a family. And everyone has to agree."

Well, I know where I can get a vote for this tree.

"Asher? Do you like the tree?" I can see by the way he pauses, he doesn't want to answer. "Dad?"

Now everyone's shaking their heads and I don't know why. It's a tree. It's not the best, but it needs love.

"Every year, Mila would pick the saddest tree in the lot and that would be our tree. She always felt bad that no one wanted it, just because it didn't look pretty or wasn't perfect."

Well, when he puts it like that… that sounds like I

like only the sad broken trees. I don't. I love the others too. Just this one needs someone.

"Ah, Mila. That's a beautiful story. And I think we should get it." My heart goes wild in my chest. She wants the tree. It will have a home for Christmas.

"And we will pick a second tree. So we can have two trees."

Now I'm deflated. That hadn't been what I meant by it. Even though my ugly tree will have a home for Christmas now.

"Mila, that was your mother." Dad pauses. The look on his face isn't good. "She wants you home for Christmas." And now my heart sinks and I no longer want to be out tree shopping.

"But she hasn't called me since I got here, dad. How is that possible? I'm not going back there." Asher wraps his arm around my shoulder in a comforting, friendly gesture, but it's so hard.

"I told her she can talk to my lawyers. That you're having Christmas here, with our family."

Why's she doing this now? Why does she want to see me at all? She's having a new baby now, she doesn't need me or even want me.

I hate my mom.

TWENTY-FOUR
MILA

My phone rings for the tenth time in the past hour. Between my mom and Malcolm, they've been blowing up my phone.

"Aren't you going to answer that?" Cadence asks me from the floor of my bedroom. I shake my head.

"Hell no, I want nothing to do with them." But the amount of phone calls I'm getting, I'm going to have to pick up soon to get them to stop. I already tried blocking their number, but dad's phone was blowing up and he demanded that I listen to them. Maybe even go for New Year's.

I think he's scared of what they can do. Malcolm will do what mom wants, and if she wants me he will get me there.

I won't just do that. I have better places to be for New Year's. And it's not gonna be in New York with mom and Malcolm. It's going to be here.

The only thing is my dad doesn't have full custody of me. If the cops come knocking on the door, they can take me back to mom. There's nothing dad can do and I hate that.

I finish painting Cadence's nails and move over to Sadie's hand. They said they would come over and be our decoy today. So I can sneak into Asher's room and make out with him for a while. Just a little while. But the payment was a fresh manicure and that I could do.

My phone rings again, and I have a look. Private number. I hesitate to pick up. Mom probably worked out by now that I'm screening her calls.

Fuck it.

"Hello?"

"Mila, oh thank you for answering." Ugh, I sink into the carpet as I shuffle my feet under my body. *Malcolm.* At least his smarter than my mom.

"We need to talk. I need you to come home so we can all talk. Together and not over the phone."

"I don't want to come back."

There's a long pause and Malcom sighs.

"I don't want to ask you this. But something happened, and I need you to come back here. At least for a few days. That's all I ask."

"What's happened?" I sit up straighter. It's strange he can't tell me over the phone. Are the phone lines bugged?

"Is there a chance you will be here for Christmas? Or sooner?" He asks again and the sound of his voice has me worried. *Oh god.* Did he do some dodgy business deal?

"No, I'm sorry. I lived in that apartment for four years and it was hell. I'm not coming back. She's not my mother. She's just a woman who gave birth to me. And never gave a shit. I'm happy here. I have a stepmom who treats me like her own." Which makes me feel guilty every day that I'm off secretly kissing Asher.

We need to tell them, before this gets out of hand or we get caught.

"Just two days. That's all I need. I will send you first class. I'll send the ticket to you now."

Wow! He's desperate, but I'm not that crazy to go back to that bitch who calls herself my mother.

Asher opens my door, he's topless and only wearing some basketball shorts. I know what he's wearing under that… nothing. He waves at Sadie and Cadence. They both sigh as he blows me a kiss.

"Look, I have to go. Nice talking to you, Malcolm." I don't give him a chance to respond. I hang up the phone. Asher gives me a puzzled look.

"He got me on a private number. I always answer them in case it's something important."

"Your mom's still trying to get you there for Christmas?" I don't think so now. Not exactly.

I shake my head.

"I think they want to talk to me in person. That's it. Malcolm seems a little worried about someone. But that's got nothing to do with me. He's only calling on Mom's behalf."

Asher holds his hand out for me to take. I let him pull me up and I stumble into him on purpose.

"Whoops." I sneak a kiss.

"There will be plenty more of them where we're

going." He winks down at me as he leads me out of the room and into his.

I feel like a naughty kid. Going to hide in his room and sneak all the candy. But it's to sneak kisses and orgasms right now. He closes his door softly to not draw attention and grabs me.

I jump into his arms and wrap my legs around him and I take in a fist of his hair and pull his head back. Those dark eyes pierce me right through to my soul.

I kiss him, hard and fast. I love these stolen moments. They're just ours.

He saunters into his walk-in closet, and I know what he wants. We talked about this. I slide down his body. A playful smile hints at my lips. He leaves me there and I look at his blue jersey waiting for me. He said he wanted me to wear it, with nothing else on. And that's what I'm going to do.

stalk out his closet wearing only the jersey. His name is across the back. I turn around and slowly lift the hem, showing a corner of my bare ass.

"Oh fuck. Mila. I'm so hard already. You tease me too much, girl." I smirk over my shoulder at him.

"I try." I wink as I drop to my knees. He groans and shifts his shorts. I can see his erection through the fabric. There's no hiding. He's ready for me. We haven't gone this far before. I want to blow his mind and he wants to lick my pussy till I come. How can I deny someone who wants to do that. The carpet is soft as I slowly prowl towards him.

He leans back on the bed, bracing himself with his elbows, and I make my way up to him. My fingers snake up his leg and under the shorts. I find his cock and give it a small stroke. He moans and I shake my head at him to be quiet.

I rub my thumb through the pre-cum and bring my hand out to taste him. Sucking my thumb into my mouth, he rolls his eyes back and tries to keep quiet. I love this feeling. It's powerful to me. Sitting between his legs, tasting him. Making him wait for me. Only I can give him pleasure and I make him wait.

"Please, Mila. God." He drops his head back and palms his cock through his shorts, and I know I've given him enough torture. I sit up and pull his shorts down until his hard length springs free and I chuckle.

"God, Mila. This isn't a laughing matter. I'm gonna die if you don't put your mouth on me."

He watches me as I run my tongue from base to tip, then suck the head of his cock. Swirling my tongue around, he groans and reaches for me. Then flops his head back on the bed, covering his eyes.

Asher can't keep still. And I love the taste of him. I use my fist and suck him as deep as I can.

"Mila, fuck, you're so good. Don't stop." I try to tell him to shut up. He'll draw attention, but he just can't help himself.

I cup his balls and roll them around in my hand and he moans curse words.

"Mila?" I hear my dad call from outside Asher's door. My eyes widen and I see Asher's face as he sits up, looking at his door.

But it's too late. My mouth lets go of his cock with a pop as Asher quickly puts his dick away. Kate's standing at his door, staring at us. My dad turns from my bedroom door and sees us.

Fuck.

Kate's the first to speak.

"We were just coming to see if you wanted to do some Christmas shopping with us. But I think... I just. I... James?" she turns to my dad and he can't even look me in the eye.

We shouldn't have done this. We should have told them first.

"How long has this been going on?" He asks. He's not furious, but he's too calm.

"A while." Asher's voice cracks. He holds onto me and I'm thankful for the comfort.

"Maybe it's best you see your mom for a couple of days like she asked, Mila. Until I can wrap my head around this."

"No," I cry out. "Please don't make me go. We can talk about this."

"I love her, James. Mom. I'm not letting her go."

Dad just shakes his head.

"Mila, this isn't an option. If you want to live here. You will go see your mother. And we will work out what to do with you both once we all cool down."

"You don't even seem that upset." Asher says to dad and I see the look on dad's face. You don't want to push him any further. He's holding it back.

I have just ruined everything.

With a blow job.

TWENTY-FIVE
MILA

I get into New York just after ten in the evening. Malcolm's there to pick me up. But he says nothing to me. Not really. He tells me I have to wait until we are all together. Then he'll talk to me.

I don't give a shit about this talk. I have a headache from crying the whole way here. Can't he see my splotchy red face? And my red-rimmed eyes. Dad had been so disappointed in me as he drove me to the airport. He didn't even speak to me once. It made me feel like I let him down.

Every time he gives me trust, I break it. This time he caught me with Asher's cock in my mouth. It doesn't get any worse than a father seeing his daughter doing that to her future stepbrother.

When I get to the apartment my mom wraps me in her arms.

"Darling, I've missed you." She coos like someone who doesn't miss me at all. God, she's so fake. Her belly isn't though. She's really having a baby.

"I have a headache, I need an Advil."

Mom waddles off into her room, and I see Junior siting on the leather couch. The one I last saw him fucking a girl over.

"Hey," he nods at me and now I'm even more curious why he's here. Wouldn't he be at his mother house?

"Once you take your Advil, we will sit down and talk. It's important we do this sooner rather than later for your mother's health."

I put my hand up and shake my head.

"Please, I have just had the worst day. I need to sleep. Can we do this in the morning?" My head pounds again and mom returns with a glass of water and two white pills. Their different to the usual Advil I take. I look up at her. "I didn't have Advil, I only had a different brand."

"I have a headache too, trust me. This will be quick."

"I'll grab you something for that." Mom disappeared to get Malcolm something for his headache, and I can see he's frustrated. She must be stalling.

I take the pills and sit down beside Junior. He doesn't look at me and I guess this is bad. Are they getting a divorce?

Mom returns and gives Malcolm the pills and water and we all sit down. I close my eyes for a moment. God, these pills are strong. My headache's almost gone. And I feel really good.

"Mila?" Malcolm calls to me. I open my eyes and try sit up but I feel so exhausted. The room is a little blurry and I blink.

. . .

"*ands where we can see them. Drop the knife.*" I groan and I roll my head. My hair is pasted to my face. I'm hot and sweaty and it sticks to my lips. I let out a puff of air to get the strands from my lips.

"Hands where I can see them. Now." Who's watching a cop show so loudly? It feels like it's in the same room as me.

"Don't shoot her, it was self-defense." I crack open an eye and see my mom standing there. Three uniformed police officers standing in the room I'm in.

"Drop the knife." One yells at me and I start to panic. Who has a knife behind me? Is someone trying to kill me… *Damon?*

I look at my arm and chest, I'm covered in blood. I shuffle backwards in a panic whose blood is this?

I bump into something large. I turn to see the lifeless eyes of Malcolm staring up at me. Bile rises to my throat as I scream.

I look down in my hand, and a bloody knife drops free.

Oh my god.

I killed Malcolm.

GET THE WIN

Death and butterflies…

https://books2read.com/thewinbelleharper

BELLE'S BOOKS

PARANORMAL REVERSE HAREM

NEW MOON SERIES ~LEXI~

Twice Bitten

Blood Moon

Rising Sun

FULL MOON SERIES ~ADA~

Fallen Wolf

Torn Mate

Shifting Sun

BLUE MOON SERIES ~ INDI~ COMING 2022

Rogue Wolf

Broken Mate

Indigo Dreams

PACK KIBA NOVELS/NOVELLAS

Midnight Prince

Shadow Wolf

Wolf Karma- Late 2022

SEEKING EDEN SERIES

Dystopian/ Post Apocalyptic Reverse Harem

Finding Nova

Protecting Nova

Rescuing Harlow

Claiming Harlow

BRIDES OF THE AASHI SERIES

Alien Romance RH

Luna Touched

Brooklyn's Baggage

Quinn Inspired

Jessica's Mates

Elle Embraced

Hadley's Heroes

REBELS OF RIDGECREST HIGH

Reverse Harem ~ Enemies to Lovers

The Pact

The Lie

TBA ~ Coming December

TBA ~ Coming January

CONTEMPORARY STANDALONES

Naughty and Nice ~Christmas Novella

ABOUT THE AUTHOR

Belle is an Artist, Author, Wife and Mother.

She has an addiction to reading, notebooks, coloured pens and mint chocolate. She lives in the beautiful Australian bush, surrounded by wildlife and the smell of eucalyptus trees.

She also has a strong love for all 60's music, believes she was born in the wrong era and should have been at Woodstock.

If you would like to find out more about Belle, please come like and follow her:

Click Here to Like Belle's Facebook Page

Join Belle in her Facebook Group

Visit my website HERE

Sign up to my Newsletter to keep up to date with my new Releases, Free Books and Giveaways.

Sign Up HERE

Printed in Great Britain
by Amazon

28408177R00145